To my sisters, Nancy and Kathy.
Many thanks.

Christmastime 1942

A Love Story

LINDA MAHKOVEC

Other Books by Linda Mahkovec

The Dreams of Youth

Seven Tales of Love

The Garden House

The Christmastime Series

Christmastime 1939: Prequel
to The Christmastime Series

Christmastime 1940: A Love Story

Christmastime 1941: A Love Story

Christmastime 1943: A Love Story

Christmastime 1944: A Love Story

Christmastime 1945: A Love Story

Christmastime 1942: A Love Story
by Linda Mahkovec
...
Copyright © 2014

ISBN-10:1-946229-08-3
ISBN-13:978-1-946229-08-3

Distributed by Bublish, Inc.

Cover Design by Laura Duffy
© Colin Young/Dreamstime

Chapter 1

∾

New York City throbbed with a war-time rhythm. Its harbor bustled with ships, barges, and tug boats coming and going, its docks crowded day and night, rain or shine, with cranes lifting, hoisted cargo swinging, gangplanks teeming. Whistle blasts and cries from the stevedores competed with the banging and squealing and clanking of chains and machinery.

Overcrowded trains shrieked into Grand Central and Penn Station, bringing thousands upon thousands of young men from all over the country, many of them their first time ever leaving home. They poured off the trains with their gear confidently slung over their shoulders, faces eager and resolute. Most sported a cheerful camaraderie, though others appeared disoriented from the whirlwind months of boot camp, training, orders to deploy, and hasty goodbyes. The trains unloaded their goods, sounded their whistles, and headed out to pick up more readied men.

A steady stream of young people threaded the city at all hours – soldiers and sailors on leave, girls rushing to jobs that needed to be filled, many of them in trades that had been closed to them a short year ago. Traffic was thicker, subways more crowded, restaurants and bars fuller, and lines longer for Broadway shows and the latest movies.

The war involved everyone. People saved their grease and metal and rubber, adjusted to the shortages and rationing, rented out spare rooms to help ease the housing shortage, and bought twenty-five dollar War Bonds and twenty-five cent War Stamps.

Volunteer spotters scanned the skies for enemy planes, and air raid wardens took charge of shelters and made sure lights were out during drills. Coast Guard Sand Pounders patrolled the beaches, and Navy binoculars swept the waters for the dreaded German U-boats.

Bolstering the city's war efforts was the ever-vigilant citizen – ear cocked to detect a foreign accent, a sidelong glance at someone asking too many questions or plying a GI with too many drinks. Tension and suspicion walked step in step with excitement and determination.

The very air of the city crackled with urgency, exhilaration, and daring. Swing and boogie-woogie music spilled out of cafes and nightclubs, dance floors vibrated with the jitterbug and lindy. Life was heightened, charged with the sense that time was short. Affairs and passions must be played out on leave, or before shipping out.

No one knew who would win the war, when and if bombs would drop on their city, what horrors lay ahead. All they knew was that they had today, this minute, now – to live. And live, they did. There was money to be made and hearts to be won, ships to be built and love to be found. Promises were made, hasty marriages performed, and "Uncle Sam honeymoons" enjoyed to the full – all forays into the future, for to plan for the future was to believe that there would be one.

Wartime and Christmastime linked hands, their presence coloring the city. Military white, olive drab, and navy mixed with holiday red and green. Beneath streetlights festooned with garlands of holly and pine, gathered groups of sailors and marines. Booths selling War Bonds stood next to rows of Christmas trees for sale. Soldiers purchased hot dogs and pretzels alongside holiday shoppers buying roasted chestnuts.

Women made the most of their ration books, saving and trading stamps, in order to buy ingredients for a memorable Christmas meal – perhaps the last with their sons or husbands for a long time.

In the Art Department of Rockwell Publishing, Lillian Drooms mentally went over her shopping list. She had made her careful purchases during the week and now eagerly awaited the weekend. The casserole was ready to be popped in the oven for tonight's dinner – the first meal with her husband, Charles, in over a month. And she had all the ingredients for tomorrow's special dinner for Gino, the young merchant seaman who rented a room on the second floor, and who loved nothing more than a home-cooked meal and –

Flour! Lillian suddenly remembered, slapping her forehead. How could she forget? She would need it for tomorrow's breakfast. Waffles, with Annette's apricot jam, cherry preserves, and maple syrup – like a breath of fresh air, straight from the orchard.

Lillian sighed to think that she had to forego her summer visit to her sister's home upstate. She had so wanted to let Tommy and Gabriel run wild through the orchard, and play with their cousins. She had so looked forward to some time with Annette – helping her with the canning and jam making, sitting out on the porch in the evenings, catching up and trading advice, just like they did as girls. But the war had changed all her plans.

Another glance at the clock. She would quickly stop by Mancetti's and pick up some flour – and some oranges for the boys, if they were available. Then she would go home, slip on her green silk blouse, and wear the pearl necklace that Charles had bought her on their honeymoon. She could scarcely believe that almost a year had passed since their marriage, a year of being a family. A year of being with Charles.

She would have the casserole in the oven and the Christmas tree lit when he walked through the door tonight. He would be surprised that they had managed the tree on their own. Though trees were expensive this year, with so few men available to cut them down, she had splurged on a thick Douglas fir, and had decorated it with Tommy and Gabriel. At eleven and eight years old, the boys were still young enough to enjoy the magic of Christmas. And it was going to be a wonderful Christmas, in spite of the war – she would make sure of that.

She waited for the minute hand of the clock to make its final sweep, pushing the hour hand to five. Then she cleared her desk, said a quick good-bye to her co-workers, slipped on her hat and coat, and hurried out the door.

Posted next to the elevator was the Art Department's reminder for the war-themed poster contest – the deadline was fast approaching. Lillian frowned briefly, wishing she didn't have to participate, and then shifted her thoughts back to the weekend. December was here now, and this weekend would mark the beginning of the Christmas season for her, with the tree up, the dinner for Gino – and Charles home. Her heart beat in anticipation at seeing him again. A month apart felt like an eternity. She stood straighter and fluffed out her hair – then laughed at herself, happy that no one witnessed her primping for her husband who was still hours away.

Three floors down, in the main office of Rockwell Publishing, her friend Izzy Briggs also quick-stepped it to the elevator, where she used the opportunity to apply a fresh coat of cherry-red lipstick, the brass trim around the doors serving as a mirror. She smacked her lips twice and tried out a smile, just before the doors opened.

In the lobby, the two women emerged from different elevators and bumped into each other in their rush to leave.

"Izzy!" cried Lillian. "Where are you off to in such a hurry?"

"It's Friday. The Stage Door Canteen beckons," Izzy said with a mischievous wink. "And you?"

"Charles comes home tonight!" Lillian said, with more enthusiasm than she intended to show.

As they wove through the bustling lobby, full of employees equally eager to begin their weekend, Izzy smiled at the excitement Lillian could never suppress when it came to Charles.

"Any plans?" Izzy called over her shoulder as she pushed through the revolving door.

Lillian followed her out into the wintry air and raised her voice to be heard above the blaring horns and accelerating buses. "We're having an early

Christmas dinner for Gino tomorrow. He ships out on Sunday and will be at sea for the holidays."

"Jeez, so soon? It seems like just last week he was plucked out of the Atlantic. The kid has nerve."

Lillian nodded, not wanting to think about the close calls Gino had experienced in the past year.

"I want to give him a special sending off. You know he doesn't have much family, and he's always kind of been on his own." A warm maternal smile appeared on her lips. "It's funny how much he reminds me of Tommy – or maybe it's just that the boys are so taken with him. He's their real-life hero. Especially for Tommy. Gino is the closest thing to an older brother he has ever known. There are several servicemen renting rooms in our building, but none like Gino."

"Well, that's something good to come out of this crazy housing shortage – though three room-mates in my small flat are three too many, if you ask me," said Izzy. "But Betty has some swell dresses – that just happen to fit me."

Izzy planted herself in front of a department store window where a red print dress caught her eye. "Speaking of dresses, look at that! Perfect for a spin around the dance floor. Gee, I hope it's still there on Monday."

A handsome officer stood next to them, tapping his watch. He turned to Lillian. "Excuse me, ma'am. My watch seems to have stopped. Do you have the time?" He gave his watch another tap.

"And the inclination," murmured Izzy.

His head snapped up, taken aback by the suggestive words.

Lillian blushed and glanced at her watch. "It's 5:15."

"Thank you," he said, looking mildly confused and then hurrying away.

Lillian leaned on Izzy's arm. "Izzy!" she whispered. "He thought *I* said that!"

"I know," Izzy said with a laugh. "He looked startled at his good luck. Well, what have we here?"

She stopped in front of a War Bonds booth on the corner, and scanned the list of Hollywood and Broadway stars that would be making brief appearances over the holidays to promote the bonds.

A couple of Broadway actresses were making sales, helped out by two young soldiers manning one side of the booth. One of the GIs emitted a long up-and-down whistle. "Hey, Gorgeous!" he hollered, eyeing Izzy.

Izzy placed her hand on her chest and looked around, as if he must be speaking to someone else.

"Who, me?" she asked, blinking.

"Yeah, you. Interested in helping out ole Uncle Sam? How 'bout a bond – or at least a coupla stamps?" He elbowed his buddy and pushed back his cap, seeing that Izzy was responding to his charms and opening her purse.

"I'm already signed up through payroll. But," she added with a coy smile, "how can I possibly say no?" She reached into her purse and took out a dollar. "For God and Country," she said. She allowed his fingers to close over her hand as she offered the bill.

"Say," said the GI, emboldened by his success. "I'm off in an hour." He let his eyes travel up and down Izzy, his action and words at odds with his boyish face – as if he had seen the come-on in a movie and was trying it out. "Howzabout you and me goin' out for a cuppa coffee – or somethin'?"

Izzy jutted out her hip and placed her hand there, banishing any pretense of shyness. "I can get my own coffee, soldier." Then leaning towards him, she added, "but I might take you up on the – *or somethin'*."

The GI stood tongue-tied, as if trying to remember what came next.

Izzy burst out laughing. "Just kidding, sweetheart. But you need to work on your manners."

"Yes, ma'am. Sorry, ma'am," said the GI, his face flushing an innocent pink.

Izzy patted his hand good-naturedly and walked off, waving her stamps. "Keep up the good work, boys!"

She ran to catch up with Lillian, who had hurried away to hide her amusement.

"Poor boy!" laughed Lillian. "You made him blush."

"Which just shows he had no business talking that way," Izzy said, tucking the stamps into her purse.

Lillian tilted her head, studying Izzy, as if seeing another side to her. Izzy had been heart-broken when her longtime beau, Red, married someone else. It had taken her months to spring back to life. But now here she was, apparently enjoying her life without him. "You really are getting to be quite fresh, Izzy."

"It's all these gorgeous young men running around. Good thing for me that I'm too old for most of them. Well – here's where I turn off. Time to hand out milk and sandwiches, and dance with the soldiers."

"Say hello to Edith for me, if she's there tonight."

"The mystery woman," Izzy said with an air of romance.

"The mystery woman?"

"That's what some of the girls call her. She has that far-off look about her – not that she's unfriendly. She's quick to smile." Izzy glanced up at the sky, thinking of how to describe Edith. "No, it's more like she lives in some world of her own.

She keeps to herself for the most part – when she's not with her beau or dancing, that is."

Lillian looked up suddenly. "Edith? With a beau? And dancing? Surely not. She's a confirmed spinster – in spite of her great beauty." Lillian lowered her voice. "And she's painfully shy about her limp."

"Not the Edith I know!" laughed Izzy. "See you, Lilly. Give my regards to Charles." She started to cross the busy avenue, but spun around to add – "tell Gino I'll save him a dance when he gets back!" She waved goodbye, and was soon lost in the throbbing Manhattan crowd that was making its way up and down the dimmed-out Times Square.

Izzy must be mistaken about Edith, thought Lillian. She would have to ask Charles. And with that thought, she quickened her step, and hurried home to await his arrival.

*

At Drooms and Mason Accounting, Mason said goodnight to the employees leaving for the day. He observed his sister Edith as she adjusted her hat in the mirror above the credenza. And anyone who knew him well, such as Mrs. Sullivan, who was just pulling on her sturdy snow boots, could see the worry in his eyes.

"Plans for the weekend, Mrs. Murphy?" he asked, and then caught himself. "Sorry. Mrs. *Sullivan*. You'd think after six months I would remember."

Mason had worked with the sixty-one year old office manager for so long, that he still had a hard time adjusting to her recently changed marital status.

"I make the same mistake myself," Mrs. Sullivan chuckled. "Dinner tonight with Brendan. And we're off tomorrow to Boston to visit the family." She knew that Mason was well aware of her plans, and that it was Edith he wanted to question.

"And where are you off to, Edith?" he tried to ask casually, ruffling through a stack of papers on his desk.

Edith raised her chin to button her coat in the mirror, and gave the slightest shake of her head. "Where I'm off to every Tuesday and Friday evening." She opened her purse, took out a tube of lipstick, and smoothed a rich shade of red over her lips, and then rolled her lips together to even out the color. She then shook out a lacy white scarf from her coat pocket and wrapped it around her neck.

Mason frowned. "No need to get all dolled up to serve sandwiches," he said, wincing at the petty petulance in his voice.

Edith raised her eyebrows at him in the mirror. "Really, Robert, you're starting to sound like an old schoolmarm."

Mrs. Sullivan was used to the mild sparring between brother and sister, and smiled indulgently at Edith.

"Oh for goodness' sake, Mr. Mason, a little lipstick never hurt anyone," she said, positioning herself in front of the mirror and opening up her own tube of lipstick. She raised her eyebrows and dabbed on a bit of rose, well aware that the effect of color on her lips was quite another thing from the crimson shaping Edith's mouth.

Edith gave a burst of laughter at the playfulness of Mrs. Sullivan, her mentor and ally.

"I scc I'm outnumbered," Mason said good-humoredly. "As usual." He stood to say goodnight as both women pulled on their gloves and made a few final adjustments in the mirror. He intended to leave it at that, but at the last minute he couldn't refrain from asking – "you won't be out late, will you, Edith?"

"Oh, for God's sake, Robert!" said Edith, opening the office door to leave.

He was about to defend himself, when Mrs. Sullivan added – "Really, Mr. Mason. I was out and about at a much younger age than Edith. And that was forty years ago." The worry in his eyes prompted her to give a quick squeeze to his arm. "Have a lovely weekend. Give my regards to Susan."

Mason nodded, and forced a smile. After the door closed, he busied himself at his desk, thinking what a task it was to be in charge of a household of willful women. His sisters and mother were out at all hours, volunteering all over the city, the girls working odd shifts at their war-time jobs. He sometimes didn't know where any of them were. And now the staid Edith was taking up with an actor! He was never more surprised in his life.

The only comforting thought was that it couldn't last much longer. The actor was sure to tire and move on to other beautiful women. He just hoped Edith wouldn't get too involved, and get her hopes up. A few laughs, a few parties, was all well and good – as long as she understood that it was just a temporary lark. For all Edith's seriousness and good business sense, he feared that she was naïve at heart. And inexperienced for being almost thirty-four. He would hate to see another repeat of – well, that was all water under the bridge.

He put some papers into his briefcase, regretting his words to Edith. He knew he couldn't risk pushing her too far. He needed her at home to help with their younger three sisters, all of them far more daring. That's what worried him. Edith had always been the responsible one, the voice of reason, somewhat wistful, but self-controlled, dependable.

Ah well, he thought, shaking off his concerns. I can't go on fretting about them forever. Soon enough my own children will be grown, and then I'll have them to worry about. The twins were almost twelve now, his five-year-old would be in school next year, and the baby was already getting teeth. There was no room to be worrying about his headstrong sisters.

Thank God, Susan was of a more serene temperament. He gave a small smile to think how his wife would simply shake her head when he worried, and say something like, "let's enjoy these happy times while we have them."

With the thought of Susan foremost in his mind, he decided that it was indeed time to call it a day. He closed up the office, and headed home to her welcoming arms.

*

Mrs. Sullivan squeezed Edith's arm as they parted at the corner. "I, for one, am delighted that you're enjoying yourself. Have a lovely evening, dearie."

"I will! And I have you to thank for it," said Edith. "I never would have volunteered at the Stage Door if you hadn't persuaded me. And I've never enjoyed myself more."

"Well, I couldn't bear to think of you devoting yourself to rolling bandages night after night in the church basement. Everyone needs to have a little fun now and then. We're only young once."

Edith tossed her head back and laughed at Mrs. Sullivan's sound advice – always encouraging a blend of purpose and pleasure. "And you have a lovely dinner – hello to Brendan!" and with that she was off.

Mrs. Sullivan watched Edith depart, delighted at the new-found sense of joy about the young woman – and so stylish in her new rose-colored coat. Mrs. Sullivan was immensely gratified to think that it was she herself who helped to bring about the remarkable transformation in Edith. In the past half year or so, it was as if a veil had been lifted that had obscured Edith's beauty and charm and confidence. And now here she was, so obviously in love. Mrs. Sullivan, a latecomer herself to the comforts and joys of love, could only be happy for the young woman.

She straightened her shoulders and picked up her pace as she neared the restaurant where her Brendan awaited her.

*

Underneath the lit globe of the Stage Door Canteen, a long line of servicemen waited for the doors to open. Edith almost balked at the sheer number of impatient and ogling young men. Instead, she lifted her head and smiled at the polite greetings and touching of caps, and ignored the whistles. She knew that Kathryn Hepburn was supposed to make an appearance that night, and that all eyes would be glued to the vivacious Hollywood star.

All, except for one pair of loving eyes. Edith lowered her head to hide her smile, the natural blush in her cheeks nicely complementing the crimson of her lips as she stepped into the Canteen.

Chapter 2

Lillian lay in the soft light of morning, resting on one elbow to watch Charles as he slept. She closely observed his shadowy cheek, his angular features, the deep rise and fall of his chest. She leaned closer and breathed in the air he exhaled, trying to breathe him into her.

Almost a year of being his wife. Sometimes when he was gone, she was afraid that she was dreaming it all. But now, here it was, Saturday morning, and there he was – safe and warm next to her, in a deep sleep that he so desperately needed. The traveling and long hours left him exhausted – working with the Navy in Virginia during the week, and trying his best to keep up with the accounting firm on the few weekends he was able to come home. She hoped he would sleep the whole morning. She gently cupped his cheek in her hand, and kissed him.

The tiniest of smiles formed on his lips, and a low moan of contentment mixed with his breathing. Lillian kissed him again and nestled under his arm. Just ten more minutes, then she would get up and make breakfast.

When she next opened her eyes, it was to see Charles getting dressed, trying not to wake her.

"I was hoping you would sleep in for a change," he said.

"*Me?*" Lillian asked, sitting up in bed. "I was hoping you would sleep until noon."

He sat down on the edge of the bed and caressed her hair. "I have to go into the office for a few hours. Then the rest of my time is yours."

Lillian jumped up and quickly dressed. "Not before breakfast. I have it all planned."

From the living room came the voices of Tommy and Gabriel. "What time is it?" she asked. "I didn't think the boys would be up yet."

When they went into the living room, Tommy threw his arms up in exasperation. "About time! It's 8:30, Mom – we're starving!"

"Just give me a minute," said Lillian, hurrying into the kitchen. "I wanted to make waffles for you all this morning."

She had so carefully thought out each meal for the weekend, counting out her rationing coupons, shopping for ingredients. She had envisioned the waffles, arranged on the holiday platter, already placed on the breakfast table by the time everyone was up – and now, here it was, late, the boys hungry, Charles needing to go to the office. She opened the lower cupboard, and in her rush to lift out a mixing bowl, a large pan rolled out and clanged loudly on the kitchen floor, giving sound to her disordered haste.

"I'll help!" cried Gabriel, pulling a chair up to the counter. "I'll crack the eggs."

Tommy slouched on the couch, and covered his ears from the banging of the pan and Gabriel's hollering.

Charles buttoned the cuffs on his shirt and raised an eyebrow at Tommy, waiting for him to lower his hands. "I think you know how to fix a bowl of cereal or butter some toast, Tommy. You should give your mom a break now and then."

Tommy opened his mouth and blinked out at the room, as if discovering a new thought. "I guess I never thought of it. Mom always fixes breakfast."

He slid off the couch and went to the kitchen, but wasn't sure what to do. With Gabriel at the counter breaking eggs into a bowl, and Lillian reaching over and around him to lift out ingredients from the cupboards, it seemed that everywhere he moved he was in the way.

Lillian much preferred to cook alone in the kitchen, but both boys were now at her elbows wanting to help. She turned on the water for the coffee, and filled the coffee pot.

"Tommy, will you get out the waffle iron and plug it in? And then you and Gabriel can set the table."

She quickly whipped up the batter, and watched as Charles lifted down the plates and glasses for Tommy and Gabriel to bring to the table. She frowned ever so lightly – she had wanted to use the holiday platter and her embroidered green and red napkins. Well, she would just have to get up earlier for tomorrow's breakfast.

In a few minutes, the table was set, the waffles were cooking, and the rich scent of coffee, somehow both calming and energizing, filled the kitchen. Lillian poured Charles a cup and set it in front of him at the table.

She watched him take a sip, lean back, and sigh with pleasure – and she was filled with a surge of happiness. The last few times he was home, he was tense, on edge, and she so wanted to give him a nice, relaxing weekend.

"It will just be a moment," she said, lifting out the first batch, and setting the waffles on a plate. She glanced over at the boys now seated at the table, wishing that she would have set out their clothes last night. Tommy was wearing the frayed red cardigan that she had already patched twice at the elbows, and Gabriel had on his favorite blue pullover. Since they were little, Tommy had always preferred red, and Gabriel blue. And it somehow suited their personalities. She poured more batter into the waffle iron, vaguely wondering if she had done anything to influence their preferences. She decided she would choose some other colors when she shopped for their Christmas presents this year.

She smiled to see Gabriel so obviously happy. He sat on his knees, leaning forward in his chair, telling Charles everything that had happened to him in the last month. But Tommy had a worried look about him that she sometimes noticed, and he was cracking his knuckles – a habit he had recently developed.

"Tommy, will you get out the jam and maple syrup? Then tell your father what you did all week. Tell him about the salvage drive at school."

Since Tommy didn't seem to have anything to say about it, Gabriel launched into telling all about the competition. "We're collecting scrap metal and paper. Tommy and Mickey are on a team, but I'm helping them. And sometimes Mickey's brother Billy, but he doesn't really like to go. He said it's too much work."

Charles turned to Tommy, concerned that he had sounded too harsh earlier. Perhaps it was unreasonable to expect an eleven-year-old to fix his own breakfast. "How much have you collected so far?"

Tommy placed the jam and syrup on the table, and then slid back into his chair. "Not very much," he said, playing with his spoon. "Mostly just tin cans and newspapers."

"We're keeping everything we collect down in Mickey's basement," Gabriel explained. "Until we turn it in at school. Whoever wins the contest gets a War Bond and a blue ribbon."

Tommy suddenly sat up in his chair. "Hey, did you know that Gino is coming to dinner tonight?"

Charles took another sip of coffee and nodded. "For an early Christmas dinner before he ships out. I understand that you and Gabriel have been learning quite a bit from him about sailing."

"Yeah. He has a friend who sailed on one of those Artic convoys, going to Mur – "Tommy tried to remember the names.

"Murmansk and Archangel," said Charles. "Russian ports."

"Yeah, Murmansk. He said it's dark all winter and light all summer."

"It's way up at the top," Gabriel added, reaching his arm above his head. "By the North Pole. Gino showed us on his map."

Lillian set the plate of waffles in the middle of the table, and sat down. "Gabriel," she laughed, "Charles is in the Navy. He knows where the ports are. Don't forget, he was in the North Sea for months during the Great War."

"Gino said you freeze to death up there," said Tommy. "Solid ice. His friend said they had to cut up their blankets and sew them into vests."

Lillian had been observing Charles as he tried to engage with the boys, but now he was distracted, his mind somewhere else. He looked off, his eyebrows pinched, seeing some unpleasant or worrisome image.

Gabriel was just about to pour syrup on his waffle, when he raised his head, puzzled. "But how can they sail in ice?"

Charles smiled at Gabriel's question, once more becoming present. "There's a lot of ice up there in the winter, that's for sure. But Murmansk is a warm-water port. That means it never freezes."

"How come?" asked Gabriel.

"It has to do with ocean currents." Charles looked over at Tommy. "I have an atlas, somewhere. Maybe we can take a look at it later."

Tommy nodded, but his mind was on Gino. "I hope Gino won't be gone too long this time. He can't tell us where he's going, but I have an idea," he added mysteriously.

"Tell me," said Gabriel.

"Can't. Loose lips. You might slip and tell someone, or talk in your sleep."

"No, I won't. Besides, you would be the only one to hear me." Gabriel gave it some more thought, and added, "What if *you* talk in *your* sleep?"

Tommy ignored the question. "I'm thinking about being a sailor when I'm older." He side-scrunched his mouth in thought. "Or maybe a pilot. I haven't decided yet."

"I'm going to be an explorer," said Gabriel. "Gino showed me his postcard collection from all over the world. There's an island with real dinosaur lizards." He stretched his arms wide. "Gigantic ones!" he said, his voice tinged with fear.

"Komodo," said Charles, widening his eyes in response to Gabriel's description.

"And another island," added Tommy, "where the men wear shrunken heads around their necks." He glanced around and was gratified by Lillian's shudder of revulsion.

As Tommy and Gabriel related more tales about Gino, Charles surprised himself by feeling a little pang of regret. He wished there was more he could share with the boys about his time in the Navy. But the interviews with engineering students would not interest them, and he couldn't talk about the research and training he was involved with. He was glad the boys had such a good role model in Gino. He was a goodhearted young man, and a born storyteller.

Once or twice Lillian tried to steer the conversation to Charles, or get the boys to talk about themselves, but they wanted to recount the swashbuckling tales of Gino.

"Can we go down there now?" Tommy asked.

"Absolutely not!" said Lillian. "Gino needs the time to pack and get ready. You can go down a few minutes before dinner tonight. Besides, I need you to come to the store with me. And I promised Mrs. Kuntzman some of Annette's preserves for her holiday baking – we'll stop by there on our way."

"Okey dokey," said Gabriel.

Tommy groaned and scooped some more jam onto his plate. "Mom, I really don't think I need a babysitter anymore."

"Tommy, we've already gone over this. Gabriel is still too young to be at home alone. And it gives me peace of mind to know that you're being taken care of while I'm at work."

"I'm almost twelve! None of the other kids my age have to. What will they think?"

"You shouldn't worry about what other kids think," said Lillian. "Besides, I thought you liked going there."

"He's worried about what Amy will think," explained Gabriel. His intention to help Tommy was rewarded with a swift kick under the table.

Lillian exchanged an amused glance with Charles. "Is Amy that little girl in your class – the new one?"

"Mom," said Tommy, "she's not little. She's my age."

"Well, *I* like going to Mrs. Kuntzman's," said Gabriel. "We have fun there, Tommy. And she always makes us good food."

"Even with the rationing," added Lillian. "I don't know how she does it. Maybe next year, Tommy. We'll see what happens."

Tommy twisted his mouth in disappointment. "But no one else –"

"There's a war on, Tommy," Charles added, cutting him off. "We need to know where you are at all times."

"We never know where *you* are," said Tommy.

"Tommy!" said Lillian, setting her fork down. "That's no way to speak to your father. He doesn't have a say about when and where he must go."

Charles raised his head, thrown off by Tommy's comment. "You know I'm down in Virginia, and that I come home as often as I can." He realized that he sounded apologetic.

Tommy knew he was wrong, but pushed on as if he were right. "Mickey's dad said you didn't have to sign up. That you're too old to be drafted. You *could* be here with us."

Lillian took a quick breath, ready to reprimand Tommy, but Charles put up a hand.

"That may be true. But my experience in the last war has some value, and if the Navy wants me, then I'll do whatever it takes, and go wherever they ask." He looked from Lillian, and back to Tommy. Did they not realize the danger they were in?

"There are German U-boats just outside the harbor," he said, waving his arm in that direction. "Sinking our ships. Dropping off spies. All up and down the coast our beaches are black with oil and wreckage."

He took a deep breath, suppressing the anger that had crept into his voice. He picked up his fork and resumed eating, cutting his waffle. "We all have to do our part, Tommy. That's all I'm saying." He tried to turn the conversation back into a normal family discussion. "Just like you're doing with the salvage drive."

Tommy shrugged and reached for the maple syrup. The bottle was nearly empty and he turned it upside down and smacked the bottom.

Charles gestured to the table and smiled out at no one in particular. "A wonderful breakfast. One of the things I miss most when I'm away."

He was aware of the strained silence that followed. Had he said too much? Had he frightened them? That was not his intent. These are just kids, he thought. I'm around grown men all the time and forget how to be around children. "So, what are you boys going to do today?"

Tommy gave a puff of exasperation, as if Charles hadn't been paying any attention. "We have our scrap drive."

"I – I meant after that," said Charles.

"Then it'll be time for dinner. With Gino," said Tommy.

A sense of failure washed over Charles. He often wondered if he had what it took to be a good father. He only had a few memories of his own father to pattern himself after. And yet they were good memories, still strong – memories that helped to shape his early childhood. He remembered the feeling of being safe, of being connected to a man's world of farming and taking care of the animals. All the memories associated with his father were warm, and fresh, and real, complete with scents and color – his dad's old brown coat with the thread-bare cuffs, the sweet smell of pipe tobacco in the evenings when he –

"I'm finished, Mom," said Gabriel, scooting back his chair.

Lillian nodded that he could be excused from the table.

"Hey," said Gabriel, turning to Charles, "I made something for you at school. A pine cone Christmas tree. For your Navy office. Want to see it?"

"Sure! Let's take a look." Charles followed Gabriel into the living room, and sat down on the couch while Gabriel reached for the pine cone tree on the bookcase.

Lillian started to clear the table and shot Tommy a withering look. "Go wash up. Go on."

Tommy reluctantly got up from the table, wishing he could start the morning all over again. He slapped the wall as he went down the hallway, wondering why he always said things he didn't mean.

From the kitchen, Lillian could hear Gabriel explaining how first his class went to the park and gathered pine cones, and then they carried them back to make the trees, gluing cotton on them to look like snow.

She left the dishes in the sink and went into the living room. There was Charles listening attentively to Gabriel, turning the lopsided tree around in his hand in admiration.

Charles set the tree on the coffee table. "You've done a fine job, Gabriel. I'm going to place this right next to our family photograph on my desk. Where everyone can see it."

Gabriel beamed, puffed up by the words of praise and love.

"Okay, Gabe," said Lillian. "You, too. Go wash up."

She and Charles laughed as Gabriel, for no apparent reason, galloped away into his room, making a clicking sound as he spurred on his imaginary horse.

Charles put his hands on his knees in preparation to stand, but remained seated, as if some counterweight prevented him from rising.

Lillian noticed the gesture, and placed her hand on his shoulder. "I'm sorry, Charles. That was rude of Tommy. I don't know where he gets things."

Charles shook his head lightly, indicating that it was of no concern, and rose to his feet.

But Lillian knew him well enough to know that the words, or Tommy's tone, rather, had stung him.

"He doesn't talk about it," she said, "but sometimes I think he's afraid of what's happening with the war, what it means. He came home from school the other day and said that the father of one of his friends had been killed. And that he didn't know what to say to him. Sometimes he seems kind of lost."

Charles took in her words as he slipped on his coat. "It's easy to forget that the children feel the effects of war, too. In ways that we can't imagine. I didn't mean to take it out on him." He put his scarf on and buttoned his coat over it. "It's just that – the reports are so dire."

Lillian saw the worry in his face and wondered how she had missed it earlier. "Charles, do you think we're in danger of being invaded? Of losing the war?"

It took him a while to respond. "It's hard to say. They have the upper hand now – but we're doing our best to change that. It's a race against time, really. We have the manpower, the resources, the resolve. It all depends if we can build our ships and planes fast enough. Thank God, Hitler overstepped himself with Russia. That should buy us some time."

"Oh my God, Charles," Lillian said, putting her arms around him. "It's all so terrible. I wish so badly you were here with us."

He stiffened and pulled back somewhat.

Lillian immediately regretted her words, and lifted her face to him. "I guess I sounded like Tommy just then. Maybe that's where he gets it. I just – I miss you."

"We're luckier than most."

"I know we are," said Lillian, again seeing the weariness in his eyes. She shook off her gloom and gave a bright smile. "Will you be long at the office?"

"Mid-afternoon or so. Mason is coming in for a few hours. It's been a challenge for him. For all of them. With so many of the staff gone. Thank God we hired Edith and some of the others when we did. She's taken over the management of accounts, allowing Mrs. Sullivan to go back to her regular work. It was getting to be a bit much for her."

"Speaking of Edith," said Lillian, clutching at the change of subject, "Izzy told me something interesting yesterday. You know she sees Edith now and then at the Stage Door Canteen, and she said that Edith has quite changed."

Charles smiled. "That was Mrs. Sullivan's doing. I'm glad it's worked out. I guess Edith stays in the background, fixing sandwiches, helping out with the decorations."

"No, Izzy said she dances with the service-men – can you believe it? And that she's walking out with someone."

"Edith?" Charles considered this, and then shook his head. "I think Izzy must be mistaken. Edith is a bit of an old maid, I'm afraid – nose to the grindstone. Though I haven't seen her in months. I suppose it's possible." He briefly recon-sidered it, and again shook his head. "No. I think Izzy must have someone else in mind."

He kissed Lillian goodbye and wrapped his arms around her in a loose embrace. "Anything you want me to bring home?"

"Some sherry or port would be nice, for later. Wouldn't it be nice to have a fire, and sit in front of it as we used to?" Though she held him in her arms, she felt that some part of him was absent, was somewhere else.

"I'll see what I can find." Charles looked down at her sweet, hopeful face, and reluctantly left the apartment.

He was grateful that she was still holding on to the way things used to be. The future was uncertain, and he felt that while he was away, she was here protecting the life they had created for themselves. He wanted their old ways to survive for as long as possible.

Though he hated to be away from her, he believed in the work he was doing with the Navy, and didn't mind the long hours. In fact, he was eager to get back. The technology he was involved with was sure to help, if it could be perfected soon enough. He had heard of radar in the 20s – but it had remained largely theoretical. The British were far ahead with the technology, though Hitler also had knowledge of it. Charles wished there was more he could do. He was busy visiting campuses and recruiting the best minds; exciting, promising work was being done at MIT, Purdue, and elsewhere.

The only thought that gave him a stab of sorrow was that sooner or later he would have to leave Lillian, and return to some of the same places he had been to in the first war, in order to observe certain findings aboard ship. But he had faith that the technology could potentially turn the tide. And the sooner the war was over, the sooner he could finally be a husband to Lillian, and a father to the boys.

He rode the subway deep in thought about his family. He kept thinking of Tommy. Poor kid needed a father around. No wonder he took to Gino. Charles grew increasingly upset with himself. Home for less than a day and already he had snapped at Tommy twice. He had so wanted to give them all a different life. A place of their own. Family trips and time together. He wanted Lillian to give up her job and stay home – though that was a point of contention between them. His brow furrowed as he realized that after nearly a year of being married, she was still a mystery to him. Was it some shortcoming in himself? He had hoped that by becoming a family, she and the boys would feel safer, happier, more secure in general. Sometimes he wondered if he was making things worse for them all.

Across from him, a couple of fresh-faced young soldiers were trying to convince a group of girls to join them for a night on the town. Not more than boys. They were someone's sons and brothers. He felt a strengthening of resolve. As much as he wished he could be home with Lillian and the boys, even more, he wanted the shipping lanes to be safe. Too many ships were being lost – too many lives.

He knew that part of this morning's tension, on his part, stemmed from the mention of Murmansk. Every time he thought of the summer's disastrous convoy PQ17 he was filled with anger and sadness. Thirty-five ships, and only eleven had made it to Murmansk. The rest were sunk. He envisioned the North Atlantic as a cold, watery graveyard for sailors, the ocean bottom littered with ghost ships. A graveyard robbed of any peace by the flitting dark shadows of the U-boats above. Stealthy, silent. Like glutted, smirking vultures circling over the abandoned carcasses on which they had lately sated their revolting appetite.

His jaw clenched as he thought of the term the Germans used to refer to their U-boat success: The Happy Time. Those cursed wolf packs. Hundreds of Allied ships sunk in a single year, many of them merchant ships. Adventuresome boys like Gino, who never had war in mind when they signed up with the Merchant Marines. Charles winced in pain at the staggering loss of lives.

He walked to the office, oblivious of the world around him. Still thinking of the troubles in the North Atlantic, he was surprised to find that the lights were already on when he walked into the office.

"Good morning, sir!" said a cheerful Mrs. Sullivan.

Her smiling face and brisk demeanor dispelled the dark thoughts, and pulled Charles up from the black underwaters of the North Atlantic, and into the sunlight and air.

"Mrs. Sullivan! What are you doing here – on a Saturday?" he said, clasping her hand, delighted to see her.

"Welcome home, sir. I thought I'd come in for a few hours, in case you and Mr. Mason should need me."

"Splendid! You look well. And how is Brendan?"

"Behaving like a man half his age!" said Mrs. Sullivan, as if criticizing her husband, but her voice brimmed with pride. "Busy at the shipyard, and squeezing in a few nights a week to play Santa at the department store."

Charles draped his coat over a chair and set his hat on a nearby desk. He felt buoyed by her energy and enthusiasm and, for the second time that morning, realized how much he missed his old life. He glanced around the office, at the business he had started almost twenty-five years ago. After the last war.

"How are things faring here?" he asked, determined to embrace the happiness offered by others, and reciprocate as best he could. "Running smoothly, I understand."

"Yes, indeed. Mr. Mason and I have everything under control. In large part, thanks to Edith. I really think she could run the whole show," she added with a chuckle.

The door opened and Mason walked in, his eyebrows raised in surprise.

"Good morning, Mr. Mason!" said Mrs. Sullivan. "We were just talking about you."

"All good, I'm sure. Well, I thought I'd be the first to arrive. Hello, sir," he said, shaking hands with Charles. "Good to see you again."

Mason hung up his hat and coat, and rubbed his hands together. "I'm afraid it's going to remain cold in the office, what with the fuel rationing. Virtually no heat on the weekends – and winter has now begun in earnest."

Charles waved the concern away, and decided to send them both home as soon as he could.

Mrs. Sullivan buttoned the long gray cardigan she now kept in the office, and then clasped her hands as if she just had a wonderful idea.

"Now! How about a nice pot of coffee to warm us up and get us through the morning?" Gratified by the cheerful responses from both men, she hurried off to plug in the electric percolator.

"Mrs. Sullivan was just singing the praises of Edith."

Mason tried to hide the pride he felt that his sister had worked out better than anyone could have expected. "Under the tutelage of Mrs. Sullivan she has done surprisingly well."

"And how are you doing, Mason? How's your wife and the rest of your family?"

"Very well, thank you. The children are excited about Christmas. My mother and sisters are out at all hours, busy with war work and volunteering. I don't think I've ever seen them so charged up."

Charles smiled, envisioning Mason's vivacious mother and sisters running circles around Mason.

"Lillian told me that Edith is enjoying her work at the Stage Door Canteen. I knew Mrs. Sullivan had encouraged her to volunteer there, but I honestly didn't think she would take to it." Charles noticed an uncharacteristic tightness form around Mason's mouth.

"Yes," said Mason. "Apparently, she quite enjoys the excitement of the Stage Door. She seems to have boundless energy these days."

"That's a good thing, isn't it?"

"I'm not so sure. She's never home anymore. Not that there's anything wrong with that. It's her life. But I understand she's been seeing an actor." He raised his head and acknowledged Charles's surprise. "I thought she had more sense. There have been several eligible men interested in her – in spite of – well..." Mason shook his head in disbelief. "Actors are an unreliable lot, at best. Here today, gone tomorrow. She met him there at the Canteen. A fellow volunteer."

"Well, that says something commendable about him, doesn't it?"

"She's setting herself up for disappointment and heartache," said Mason, a look of anxiety in his eyes. "I don't want that to happen."

"No, I understand how you feel. But Edith has a good head on her shoulders. I'm sure she'll act sensibly, move on to more solid ground."

Mrs. Sullivan's humming and clicking of spoons and cups caused Mason to lower his voice. "Don't let *her* hear," he said, gesturing towards the pantry. "She's quite taken Edith's side in this whole thing. Thinks Edith can do no wrong. Much as I love my sister, I do think Mrs. Sullivan gives her too much credit. I know Edith better that she does, after all. For all Edith's confidence here at the office, I'm afraid when it comes to men she's quite naïve."

Mason studied the floor, following some internal dialogue. "True, she's capable, reliable. But there's another side to her – more, I don't know how to describe it – dreamy." He nodded, as if he had hit upon the right word, and a faint smile softened his face. "She used to write poetry, and took dance classes, wanted to travel, had all sorts of dreams and ambitions."

"You mean before – " Charles felt somewhat uncomfortable talking about Edith's personal life.

"Before the polio," said Mason, sensing that Charles was reluctant to say it. "It hit her in her early twenties and all her dreams came to an end. Though perhaps that had less to do with the illness, and more to do with – " He stopped mid-sentence, and hesitated before finishing his thought. "She had her heart broken." He looked down, and whatever memory crossed his mind strengthened his resolve.

"No," he repeated. "I can't let some fool of a man do that to her again."

Mrs. Sullivan's arrival prevented any further discussion of the matter. She stepped briskly out of the pantry and set a tray on the side credenza.

"Here we go, then," she said, arranging the coffee pot, mugs, and a plate of biscuits. She was the only one to know that the biscuits, coffee, and sugar were happily purchased with her own ration coupons.

Chapter 3

෨

After being pestered all afternoon, Lillian finally gave in to Tommy and Gabriel and let them go downstairs to visit Gino before dinner.

Tommy now sat at the foot of the bed, flipping through Gino's postcard collection, while Gino packed his duffel bag.

Gabriel stood on a chair, looking at the wall map with red pins marking the places Gino had sailed to. Gabriel let his finger journey from port to port, reading off some of the names as he moved from one side of the map to the other.

"Bombay, Cape Town, Rio de Janeiro, Hong Kong, Shanghai. Wow, Gino! You've been everywhere." When he reached the edge of the map, he leaned in closer to puzzle over a word, and then put his fists on his sides. "Huh! I didn't know there was a Fic Ocean."

Tommy got up to see what nonsense Gabriel was talking, and on seeing it, howled with laughter, rolling back onto the bed.

Gabriel looked from Tommy and back to the map. "What? It says Fic Ocean, right here."

Gino rumpled Gabriel's hair. "You goofball. That's the other half of this," he said, pointing to the far right side of the map. "Paci-"

Gabriel raised his eyebrows as he read the other half of the word. "Ohhh!" he laughed, realizing his mistake.

Gino took out a few small items from his top drawer, and placed them into a bag, while giving Tommy some last minute advice.

"So Tommy, how's she gonna know you're interested if you don't tell her? Or at least show her?"

Tommy winced. "But – what if she laughs? I hardly know her."

Gino was quiet for a few moments, then he suddenly snapped his fingers. "Hey, how about something with school? Maybe you could study together."

Tommy's face scrunched up in doubt. "I haven't even really talked to her yet."

"Or how about asking her to help with your scrap drive?"

Again Tommy frowned at the suggestion and shook his head. "The girls have their own teams. She's doing a book drive. Besides," he said, rolling

Linda Mahkovec

back on the bed in defeat, "we're doing terrible. I thought – well, I was hoping that maybe if we won the prize, then she might – you know, kind of notice me. And maybe then I could – say something."

"Tommy, Tommy, Tommy," said Gino, putting one foot on the chair and folding his arms over his knee. "You got it all backwards."

Tommy and Gabriel recognized this position as Gino's story stance, and that he was about to launch into a tale. Tommy sat up, and Gabriel jumped off the chair and onto the bed next to Tommy.

Gino waited for them to get settled and rubbed his chin, deep in thought. "You're what – eleven now?"

"Almost twelve," said Tommy.

"That's old enough."

"I'm eight," offered Gabriel.

Gino considered this and gave a slow nod. "A little information won't hurt you, either."

Gabriel brightened at being thought old enough for Gino's advice.

"You like this girl, right? This Amy?"

"Yeah," answered Tommy, beginning to twist the button on his shirt. "I mean – she seems nice. I don't really know."

"She's real pretty," said Gabriel. "And real smart. She wears glasses and red socks. And she always says hi to me."

"That's a good sign."

Gabriel smiled up at Tommy, sure that this time he was helping him out.

"So. Here's the plan." Gino held up a finger. "One. You gotta let her know you exist. Talk to her. Ask her about where she used to live. Ask her about her family. Ask her anything – just get talking."

Gino put up another finger. "Two. Invite her to somethin'. Ask her to the soda fountain. Ask to walk her home." A third finger went up.

"Three. After you accomplish points one and two. It's Christmas. Get her a present."

"A present?" asked Tommy. "I wouldn't know what to get a girl."

Gino winked. "That's the clincher. You gotta get her somethin' special that shows you've been listening."

"How will I know what that is?" asked Tommy.

"By starting with – " he held up his index finger again and waited for Tommy to answer.

"One! Talk to her!" shouted Gabriel.

"Shut up, Gabe," said Tommy.

"Hey, hey – that's no way to talk to your brother. He's on your side. You need all the help you can get in life. Trust me. And when you find that special girl…"

Gino stared off, his face all dreamy and happy, as if seeing something agreeable.

Gabriel followed his gaze to the blank wall, and then back to Gino.

Gino sighed. "Did I ever tell you about the first time I saw Anna Mae?"

Both boys shook their heads.

"The first time I saw Anna Mae, I felt like I was sucker punched in the heart. No kiddin'. I just stopped and stared as she walked past me. There I was, visiting my grandparents, outside of Philly, checking the mailbox for them at the end of the sidewalk. It was a patchy fall day, leaves blowin' all around, big, big puffy clouds in the sky. Trees all orange and yellow and red. I was just thinkin' what a nice day it was, the kind of day that makes you happy just to be alive – when all of a sudden, this beautiful girl came walkin' towards me." Gino waved his arms around in vague shapes, as if trying to recreate the vision. "She was wearing a blue checked dress, and a white sweater – carrying a bag of groceries. I stood there with my mouth open as she approached. Then she passed by, turned her head to me – and smiled! I watched her until she entered the house down the street."

It took Gino a moment to leave the vision and return to Tommy and Gabriel. "And what did I do?"

Gabriel opened his hands and shrugged his shoulders high.

Tommy opened his mouth – here it was. The secret.

Gino bunched his lips in disgust. "I turned and went back inside! What a dope! I thought about her night and day for the next week, replaying that morning over and over and over. I just kept thinkin' she was so pretty and bright and lovely, and I'm just ole Gino, your average swabbie, and she'd never be interested in me. And I'm frettin' and stewin' and dreaming of her, thinkin' what I could say to her." He rolled his eyes. "Jeez, I even started writing poems."

Gabriel likewise rolled his eyes and grinned. Tommy started to crack his knuckles, hoping the answer didn't involve poetry.

With the back of his hand, Gino gave a light swat to Tommy's shoulder, to make sure he was paying attention. "Then I grabbed a hold of myself – by the collar so to speak – and gave myself a good shake. And I says – Gino. Be bold! Stop wasting precious time and go over there and ask that girl if she'd like an ice cream soda. I told myself – Be bold. If you fail, you fail."

Then his face shone with happiness. "And then it hit me! If I fail, all that means is – I get another chance to try again! Well, that sort of cheered me, puffed up my sails. All I wanted was plenty of chances with Anna Mae. I realized I couldn't lose." Gino stared off again, smiling.

Tommy and Gabriel exchanged glances, knowing the ending, but wanting to hear it all the same.

"So, what happened?" asked Tommy.

"Were you bold?" asked Gabriel.

Gino burst out laughing. "I sure as heck was! I invited her to the soda fountain the next day, and she said yes on the spot. She later asked what took me so long."

For the first time, Tommy appeared cheered.

"Now here it is. A year later. And...well, I guess I can tell you two – my first and second mates. We're gonna get married as soon as I get back."

Gabriel widened his mouth and eyes in happy expectation, but Tommy became a little disconcerted. That was taking things too fast.

Gino swung the chair back under the desk and addressed Tommy. "So, my advice to you is: Be bold. You can't lose. If she says no, you move on to phase two. You try again, or you regroup and rethink the whole thing. Either way, you're a step ahead, instead of wallowing in despair. Make sense?"

"Yeah," Tommy said shyly, looking down. He tried to envision such boldness in himself.

"Now, come on! Chow time. Dinner's waiting at Chez Lillian."

Gabriel turned a quizzical face to Gino.

Tommy puffed up his chest and explained. "That means *house* in French. Gino taught me lots of French words – like *oui oui*, and *oooh lala*. And *snafu*."

Gino gave a little cough. "That last one's not exactly French."

"You said 'pardon my French' when you explained what it means."

"What does it mean?" asked Gabriel. "Tell me."

"I'll tell you some other time." Gino gave a side wink to Tommy, indicating that there were certain things that Gabriel was still too young to hear. He grabbed the small bag, and steered the boys out of the room.

"Come on, mates. Your mom is fixin' a special going away Christmas meal for me. I can't be late for that!"

He then started to whistle a popular tune that Tommy and Gabriel picked up on and sang all the way upstairs to their apartment. "You're a sap, Mr. Jap, you make a Yankee cranky!"

From the kitchen Lillian heard the boys clamoring up the stairs. "Quick, Charles!" she called into the living room. "Plug in the tree lights!"

Tommy and Gabriel burst through the door with Gino.

"We're here!" cried Gabriel.

Charles greeted them at the door and shook Gino's hand.

"Come on in, Gino!" called Lillian, stirring the gravy on the stove. "Make yourself at home."

Gino took a deep whiff, and walked into the kitchen. "Boy, does that ever smell good!"

"It will just be a few more moments." Nothing made Lillian happier than to have her cooking appreciated. "Tommy, Gabriel – come help me in the kitchen while Gino visits with your father."

Charles showed him into the living room where a small fire was burning brightly. The mantel was hung with the boys' stockings, and Lillian's collection of Victorian Christmas cards was arranged above them. The scent of pine from the Christmas tree filled the small room and its colored lights added to the feeling of festivity.

Gino leaned back, indulging in the comforts of a real home. Within seconds he and Charles were deeply engaged in talk of the war, Charles rapt with attention at Gino's vivid descriptions of the things he had seen, and of the close calls he had experienced.

Charles felt his mood lighten as he listened. Gino had a way of describing everything with a sense of humor and excitement, mixing stories of danger with the antics of his fellow sailors. And Gino was equally interested to hear what Charles had to say about his time in the Navy and how things had changed since the last war.

Over a lively dinner, Charles had the impression that Gino was making light of the sea journeys so as not to worry Lillian and the boys. Now, over dessert, Gino was in the middle of another of his stories about his last voyage, the boys hanging on his every word.

"Freezing cold night. A million bright stars overhead." Gino gazed up, once again seeing the firmament, and spread his arms wide. "Like a big glittering dome over the ocean. There I was, standing on the bridge. Just starting the middle watch."

"Midnight to 4:00," explained Tommy.

"That's right. Eight bells found me staring out at the dark waters, thinkin' of my girl. Don't get me wrong – my mind was focused on my duty." He enacted the sweeping, peering nature of his watch: "Eye on the sky, eye on the water; eye on the sky, eye on the water. But a part of my mind was on Anna Mae and missing her, and I worried that she was missing me. Midnight passes. And then bell one. Bell two. And I'm frettin' and stewin', and for some reason, I lifted my head high up to the stars, looking for an answer."

He leaned his head back, remembering the sense of awe. "There were so many stars, and they were so bright and beautiful! And I realized that if Anna Mae looked up, she would see the same stars. And I thought, no matter how long this war goes on, no matter where I may be, here was a way for me to be with her. And I felt such – well, it was like a feeling of peace and happiness, at the same time."

Gino looked down, and for the first time became a little shy. "And I knew then that I always wanted to be with her."

A deep silence followed, punctured by an outburst from Gabriel. "So you got bold and asked her to marry you!"

Lillian shot Gabriel a look of surprise.

Gino reached over and mussed Gabriel's hair, laughing. "That's exactly what I did. And she said yes! And we're gonna get married soon as I get back."

"Oh, Gino, that's wonderful!" cried Lillian.

Charles reached over to shake Gino's hand. "Congratulations, Gino! This calls for a toast." He stood and lifted his glass. "To Gino and Anna Mae. May you have fair winds and a following sea."

Gino's smile couldn't be any wider as Lillian and Charles clinked their glasses to his.

"And to the stars," added Tommy, raising his glass of milk.

Gino grinned over at Tommy. "Especially the middle star in Orion's belt. I figured that would be the easiest star for Ann Mae to find. I told her about that night on the bridge. And that whenever she misses me, to just look up into the night sky and find Orion's belt — and I'll do the same thing. And in that way, we'll be together."

"That's lovely, Gino," said Lillian.

"Of course, I'll have to find another constellation after winter," he added.

"Cause then Orion will be hunting somewhere else, right?" asked Gabriel.

Gino gave a wink of approval at Gabriel. "That's right. Anna Mae said she wants to learn all about the stars. So I figure this will be a good way for me to teach her. Pick a constellation for different times of the year, different voyages."

Tommy's eyes filled with concern. "Gino, when you get married, you're not going to move away, are you?"

Gabriel hadn't thought of this possibility. "You can't move, Gino," he said. "There's enough room down there for Anna Mae, too."

"You two are ten steps ahead me, as usual," laughed Gino. "We just decided last week. But don't worry. Wherever we are, it won't be too far away. I promise."

He now stood and lifted his glass. "Here's to one of the nicest families I've ever known." He cleared his throat, losing some of the ease that accompanied his storytelling. "You don't know this, but you all got me through some tough times. Some lonely times. You made me feel like I was part of your family – inviting me up to some of the best dinners I've ever had. Birthday celebrations with these two rascals," he grinned over at Tommy and Gabriel. "They're just like my real kid brothers." He lowered his head, and a shadow crossed his face.

Lillian suddenly felt apprehensive; she had never seen Gino look worried.

But he quickly cast aside the darkness and gave one of his dazzling smiles. "So I want to say thank you. And Merry Christmas! And I can't wait to get back home to Anna Mae – and to you." He raised his glass and took a sip.

Lillian thought that his eyes looked moist, but he was smiling, and putting on a brave face. How hard it must be to leave each time. Her heart went out to the brave young man, and her own eyes teared up.

"But before I go – " Gino sniffed and quickly left the table to retrieve his bag by the door. "I have something for you."

Lillian waved everyone into the living room. "Do you have time for a cup of coffee, Gino? Or another slice of pie?"

He put his hand on his stomach as if he couldn't eat another bite. "Thanks, but I have to get up in a few hours. But I can't leave without first giving you all something." He reached into his bag and pulled out two sailor caps for Tommy and Gabriel.

Both boys shrieked with delight. Tommy took his cap and ran to the mirror to try it on. "Thanks, Gino. Now I really look like your First Mate!"

Gabriel jumped up on the couch and then took a leap onto Gino's back, hooking his arms around Gino's neck. "Anchors aweigh! Land Ho! Batten down the hatches!" he cried, and then slid down Gino's back.

Gino was obviously used to such antics, because he simply laughed and pulled another item from the bag – a piece of scrimshaw that he handed to Charles. "I found it in an old odds and ends shop in Boston – down by the wharves. Thought you'd find it interesting."

"Look at that!" cried Charles, fascinated, turning it around in his hand. "I'd say it's quite old. Are you sure you want to part with it, Gino?"

"Sure. I thought you might like it."

"Can I see?" asked Tommy, reaching out for it. "This is made from whale bone, right?"

"Let me see," cried Gabriel, pushing his cap out of his eyes and leaning over Tommy. "It's a ship!"

"And for you," Gino said, addressing Lillian. He handed her a little gray box with gold lettering. "I can't thank you enough for all you've done for me. I hope you think of me when you wear it."

Lillian opened up the box and beheld a beautiful rosette brooch, clear crystal, sparkling with gold and silver and rainbow glints. "Oh, Gino! It's lovely! But you shouldn't have."

She went to the mirror and pinned it on her sweater, then turned to show Charles and the boys. "I will think of you, Gino, whenever I wear it."

"Hey!" cried Gabriel. "It kinda looks like a star! Now Anna Mae *and* Mom will think of you."

"Man, oh man! That makes me the luckiest guy in the world! To have two beautiful women lookin' at stars and thinkin' of me." He draped an arm around Tommy and Gabriel. "Well, I gotta go. You two stay out of trouble, okay?"

"Hurry back, Gino!" said Tommy.

Gino leaned over and whispered to him, "Remember: Be bold."

Tommy grinned and nodded. "I will."

"Bye, Gino. I'll be waiting for you, Captain!" said Gabriel.

Lillian took his hand in both of hers. "Goodbye, Gino. I can't wait to meet Anna Mae. I'm so happy for you both."

Gino took a step back, and looked at them all, as if memorizing the image to take with him. He swallowed, and then gave his head a firm nod.

"I'll see you out," said Charles.

Charles pulled the door closed behind him and walked Gino to the end of the hallway, wondering what, if any, advice he could give, and settled on the simplest. "Be careful out there, Gino. Don't take any chances."

"I'll be careful. But I figure a guy's luck can't last forever." He reached into his jacket and handed Charles two letters. "To my grandparents, and to Anna Mae. Just in case."

A low groan escaped Charles as he took the letters. He knew that the risks in the Atlantic were too real to try to minimize or make light of. And he knew what it was like to sail off in wartime. He slowly nodded, and clasped Gino's hand. "Take good care of yourself."

"Thanks." Gino then playfully snapped a salute, and ran down the stairs.

Charles returned to the apartment and stood a moment, taking in everything. Lillian was cleaning up the kitchen, lightly humming. He could hear Tommy and Gabriel splashing around the bathroom sink, singing an old sea shanty that Gino had taught them. For the first time it hit him hard that one day soon, he, too, would have to say his goodbyes.

He watched Lillian for a moment, and then went into the kitchen and put his arms around her.

"Come," said Lillian, turning into his embrace. "Let's sit in front of the fire."

She carried two glasses of port over to the coffee table, and then nestled next to Charles on the couch. The fire had burned down to embers, with a few small flames clinging to the coals and emitting a soft hissing sound.

"I'm so glad you were here for Gino's dinner," Lillian said, tucking her legs underneath her. "It meant a lot to him, I could tell. I think he enjoyed himself, don't you? He really has become like family over this past year."

"He's a remarkable young man. The boys have certainly taken to him," he said with a chuckle. "He's a good influence on them."

"Yes, he is." Lillian's brow creased slightly as she gazed into the fire. "Do you think he's worried? I thought he seemed a little – I don't know, subdued, in spite of his smiles."

"Well, it's always hard shipping out, leaving your loved ones behind." Charles knew that no matter what he said, Lillian would worry about Gino until he returned.

"That must be it. Especially now that he's engaged." Lillian pulled off her clip earrings and rubbed her earlobes. Then she leaned back and gave a sigh of pleasure. "I've missed this. Evenings in front of the fire. Quiet times together with you." She turned to face Charles. "I didn't even get a chance to ask you how everything was at the office today."

Charles put his arm around her shoulder as she leaned into him. "Oh, fine. Mason has everything under control. Mrs. Sullivan was there, making coffee for us, running out to get sandwiches for lunch." He reached forward, and took a sip of port. "Oh, by the way," he said, setting the glass back down, "apparently you're right about Edith. Mason said she loves her work at the Stage Door Canteen. And she does indeed have a beau. An actor."

"No! Really?" Lillian sat up, her eyes brightening at the idea of Edith having someone. "How wonderful!"

"Mason doesn't seem to think so. He's concerned about her."

"But why? Has he met the man?"

"He has no intention of doing that. He obviously doesn't expect it to last. An actor, and all," he said, merely repeating Mason's words.

Lillian pulled her chin in and fixed her eye on Charles. "For heaven's sake, Charles. That sounds quite patronizing. What does it matter what profession he has?"

Charles hadn't really given it any thought, and Lillian's choice of words took him aback. "I don't know. It's none of my business, after all."

"Surely Mason has more faith in his sister than that. She's not the type of woman to act foolishly, I should think."

"I don't know all the particulars. I only found out about it today."

Lillian got up to stir the embers, and then returned to the couch, keeping her eyes fixed on the low flickering flames. "I can see an actor, or an artist of some sort, being interested in Edith. Can't you? You have to admit that she's beautiful. She has an old-fashioned quality about her that sets her apart from other women."

"I suppose so," said Charles. "On the other hand, there's a guardedness, an aloofness, that I think might put men off. Men like warmth and liveliness in a woman, especially in times like these."

He took her hand, trying to get back the closeness of just a minute ago.

"Perhaps," said Lillian, gazing into the fire. "But I think some men would find her ravishing. There's an ethereal quality, mixed with sensuality, that someone of an artistic nature would be drawn to." She picked up her glass and took a sip. "It's a shame Mr. Mason isn't more accepting of them."

"Well, I think he's preoccupied these days. He has his hands full with a household of women – four sisters, and his own wife and children. And his mother. He makes her sound like the spirited ringleader – encouraging them all to spread their wings. I wouldn't have been surprised if it had been one of the younger ones taking up with an actor. You've met them. They're quite a lively bunch."

Lillian smiled at the thought of the three younger sisters, all vivacious and engaging.

"But Edith," continued Charles. "She has the same reserve as Mason – you never really know what's going on inside of them."

"Sounds like someone else I know," Lillian said, kissing his cheek.

Charles drew her to him. "Enough about everyone else," he said, waving his hand against the intruders. "I want to hear about you. How's life at the publishing house?"

"Oh, fine. Mr. Rockwell drives us all pretty hard. There's such a demand for posters, magazine covers, illustrations. I'm learning so much. My only complaint is that Mr. Rockwell has me drawing the same *dame*, as he refers to her, over and over again – except that her dress keeps getting shorter. War Production Board restrictions, he keeps reminding us." She raised and dropped her eyebrows in doubt of Rockwell's motivation. "Anything to increase sales."

Charles gave a quiet laugh at Lillian's ongoing criticism of her boss.

"He's sponsoring a war poster contest and I have to come up with something soon. There's going to be a panel of judges – three outside artists. And Rockwell, of course. 'Give me something with meat on it!' he said. 'Make 'em feel! That's what sells!'"

"Aren't you pleased at the opportunity?"

"I don't know," she said. "I'm having a hard time with it, for some reason. The Art Department teases me that my work is too soft. Too sweet. They say that Rockwell wants harrowing explosions, heroic deaths, high drama." Lillian took a sip and shrugged.

"I'm sure you'll come up with something."

Lillian knew his response was supposed to be comforting, but it somehow sounded trivializing. "I suppose so," she said, not wanting to discuss it any further.

"And there's nothing wrong with being soft and sweet," he added.

Lillian started to defend herself against the words she always interpreted as meaning ineffectual and insipid. But she decided to keep quiet.

Charles noticed Lillian's lips pressed together, the sudden tenseness about her, and thought that perhaps she felt overwhelmed by her job. He knew that Rockwell could be a difficult taskmaster. He hesitated a moment before bringing up the subject that always ended in a stalemate.

"Wouldn't it be nice to be able to draw what you want, when you want?" He waited for Lillian's response, but she just stared into her glass.

"Have you thought more about it?" he asked.

"You mean give up my job," she said, aware of the sharpness that had entered her tone. "Charles, you know how hard it was for me to get this position. I'm finally earning money as an artist and I'm not about to give it up. At least for the time being, I want to work."

"I'm not saying to give up being an artist. But you would have more time *as* an artist if you didn't have to work."

"And I explained that the time is just not right. I want to keep working. I need to stay engaged with an operating art department in order to keep growing. I've explained this again and again. I don't know why you're always so against it. It's as if you don't really take me seriously as an artist."

Charles opened his mouth. That was not his sentiment at all and he found himself on the defensive again. "Of course I do! And I'm not against it. That's not it at all. But – it would be nice to know that you were safe at home."

He gave a weary sigh, and wondered if he sounded patronizing again. "That's all I'm saying." He suddenly became aware of how physically tired he was.

She leaned away from him and set her glass on the coffee table. She knew she had overreacted, but this was something she felt strongly about.

Charles tried to shift the conversation to the boys, to the rationing books. Lillian mentioned something about the weather, and the Christmas cards that had arrived. But something had come between them and stubbornly remained there.

They sat quietly for another ten minutes, watching the fire slowly sputter out.

Then Charles stood and held his hand out to Lillian. "Let's go to bed. I think we're both tired."

Chapter 4

⁓

Edith sat at the edge of her bed, rubbing rose-fragranced lotion into her hands and arms. It was well past midnight. It must be close to 2:00, she thought. She had come home and taken a hot bath, grateful that the bathroom was at the end of the hall. She didn't want to disturb anyone; she knew that sometimes Susan had a hard time getting the baby to sleep.

A pool of golden lamplight illuminated her velvet robe, one of her treasures from the antique store near Desmond's place in the Village. They had come upon the shop one afternoon and she had immediately fallen in love with the place. The proprietor had appreciated the way the Victorian blouses fit Edith so flatteringly, and he encouraged her to try on several. Edith had purchased one of the lacy high-necked blouses, along with a gray striped Edwardian skirt. When Desmond spotted the garnet-colored robe, rich with gold and black embroidery twining up the sleeves and blooming into foliage around the shoulders, he had insisted on buying it for her. He said it conjured up images of desert caravans and moonlit oases, of someplace ancient and faraway. For some unfathomable reason, Desmond considered her exotic. Edith gave a small laugh at his romantic notion.

From under her pillow, she took out a small notebook and opened it on her lap. She had taken up her old habit of filling pages with images and words, something she hadn't done for years. Phrases or a few sketchy lines to express some glimpse of a thought or feeling or mood. Sometimes a poem would take shape; sometimes patches or smudges of color would dominate the page, with a few single words interspersed. Always fragmentary, collage-like. Her old, dreaming self, that found such meaning in everything, had reawakened. Lately, she found herself once again stepping over the threshold into that other world, and tentatively exploring, gathering small beauties to take back with her to the day-to-day world.

She opened the drawer to her nightstand and reached for her tin of oil pastels. She lifted the lid, and ran her fingers over the colors, choosing deep Prussian blue and cobalt, gold, silver, and umber. Then she began to draw, her fingers trying to capture the image in her mind. A sketch emerged of two large pillows, a rumpled comforter, a soft bed under a large window. The night world outside dotted with stars. *Colors of midnight*, she wrote beneath it. She studied the bed, and added a few more lines, and then sprinkled a dusting of stars onto the pillows and blanket. Satisfied, she tucked the notebook back under her pillow and turned off the lamp.

The early sketches in the notebook were shadowy, vague. But over the past several months, the images had gradually become clearer, beginning with the drawings of a castle against a darkening sky, stone steps, a man's gauntleted hand reaching out to a cloaked figure. Drawings from one of her early days spent with Desmond. A friend of his worked at the Astoria Signal Corps learning the art of film-making, producing war-related instructional and informational films for the government. One day, he had asked Desmond and a few other friends to enact some scenes from Shakespeare while he filmed and took photographs.

They had congregated at the Belvedere Castle in Central Park on a chill and cloudy spring evening. The film-maker wanted the stairs, and height, the distant vistas, the castle suggestive of another time.

Edith had been intensely curious about everything, and loved watching Desmond in different roles. His sword fight, his lines delivered at the edge of the wall, his tragic death on the stairs that was all too believable. As soon as the camera moved away, she had run and knelt down beside him, placing a hand on his cheek. He had laughed and pulled her to him.

The director, captivated by Edith's beauty and spontaneity, had tossed her a cape, and began to give her directions. Though usually shy, Edith had playfully donned the cape, easily slipping into the world of make-believe. The director had her furtively climb the steps and then glance over her shoulder, the camera capturing the haunting quality of her face, her striking profile and deep-set eyes.

That was long months ago. So much had changed since those early, tentative days.

Tonight she had attended a cast party with Desmond. He had been worried that she wouldn't like it, but he wanted her to meet the cast, and, moreover, he wanted them to meet her. She was a bit uneasy at first, but there was such a sense of camaraderie and sheer exuberance, that she soon got caught up in it all and immensely enjoyed the evening.

Aside from their nights at the Stage Door Canteen, most of their time together was spent alone. So tonight she had enjoyed seeing different sides of him, like facets that caught various lights – at one moment his leaning forward all rapt with attention, then sudden bursts of laughter at some comment or story, then a far-off look; but always connected to her – his hand on her leg, giving a light squeeze or a caress, an attentive filling of her glass, an arm draped over her shoulder, or just a gaze into her eyes that momentarily shut out everyone else. Afterwards, they had gone to his place – his cramped, charming, gypsy caravan-like rooms. And later, they had taken the train uptown – and then the slow walk to her home in the soft-falling snow. A magical night.

She nestled into the comfort of the pillows and blankets, floating in the sweet sensation of well-being. The hot soak in the bathtub had dissolved the achiness in her feet and legs, and banished the cold of the night.

The rose-scented lotion was a gift from Desmond, and the scent of it now formed a soft cloud of memory around her. She felt the alluring pull of slumber, but fought it off – put up a gate against sleep.

For she wanted to replay her time with Desmond, like a bedtime fairytale that she told herself every night. She would start at the beginning and see how far she could get in their story.

It had all started in the spring, after weeks of indecision about whether she should volunteer at the recently opened Stage Door Canteen. She had finally allowed Mrs. Sullivan to convince her to sign up as a Junior Hostess. At first she had been terribly uncomfortable with all those vibrant young women and innumerable men. Thank God for Lillian Drooms and her friend Izzy. Lillian, knowing that she was hesitant about going to the Canteen, had invited them both to dinner one evening to introduce them. Izzy, a volunteer at the Stage Door since its opening, was wonderful – funny, irreverent, protective, adventurous. She knew everyone. It was Izzy who had first acquainted her with some of the actors who volunteered there. When Izzy introduced her to Desmond Burke, Edith felt that her legs were going to buckle. A tall, handsome man – with a quiet intensity that hinted at worlds of richness inside.

He had beheld her with a peculiar expression, as if she were some strange bird who had just alighted in front of him. Did she strike him as odd? Perhaps she should have taken her sisters' advice and worn one of their dresses. But she was uncomfortable in the shorter hems.

She had felt herself blush, and quickly shifted her attention to the other actors Izzy was introducing.

Then later that night, when she was finally feeling somewhat at ease, at least able to give yes and no responses to the soldiers' questions, she had looked around for Desmond Burke and caught him staring at her. He gave a small smile that she suspected resulted from sympathy. He must have noticed my limp, she thought, prickling at the idea. If there was one thing she couldn't tolerate, it was a look of pity. She had abruptly turned away from him – then, and every time she caught him looking at her.

Izzy had dropped a few bits of information about all the actors there. She said that Desmond was unattached. That he had married long ago, but that his young wife had died in childbirth. That he was from a family of actors, on stage since he was young.

In the following weeks, from an obscured position next to a pillar, or across the ever-crowded dance floor, Edith observed him. He was kind and generous to the soldiers, with the air of an older brother – indeed, he seemed a good twenty years older or more from most of the servicemen. And when, to her alarm, he happened to catch her watching him, his whole manner seemed to express a sudden happiness.

What could he mean? Or was she simply seeing things? Afraid of the feeling that was stirring inside her, and not wanting to be the recipient of anyone's pity, she gave up her shifts for two weeks, convincing herself that she was better off rolling bandages. But something drew her back to the Stage Door. She told herself that he was just a kind man, and had no interest in her. Of course he didn't. And so she had returned.

And when she did, he finally spoke to her. She found herself stationed next to him at the sandwich counter.

"I was afraid you were not coming back," he had simply said.

And that had begun their friendship. He later told her that he had switched stations with some-one in order to be next to her that night. And that he was somewhat afraid of her, which caused her to burst into laughter.

At first she didn't take it all seriously. She enjoyed his company, and loved watching him on stage, loved the seriousness he brought to every-thing – serious, yet warm and caring, with a deep laugh that melted her.

But over the months, he had eased open her world, making her realize how closed she had been to life. It was Desmond who coaxed her to dance with the soldiers – she who hadn't danced in years; Desmond who took her to the theater and out to clubs and parties; and Desmond who slowly opened her heart. In the quiet evenings in his apartment, they cooked meals together, and talked long into the night, hungry for details of each other's life, curious to know the depth and breadth of each other's mind, weaving their lives and souls closer and tighter.

Lately he spoke about marriage. She had neither agreed nor disagreed – she was simply astounded that it was even a possibility for her. At first the idea existed only in the imaginative, dream part of her life, like the images in her notebooks, in that world of longing and beauty. But slowly she was coming to believe in the vision. She could imagine coming home to Desmond, cooking for him, going to his rehearsals after work, blending their lives together.

He even surprised her by saying that perhaps it was not too late for them to start a family. Make a home together. His parents had both been actors and they had traveled widely, and the actor's life was normal to him. Was that something she could see for herself? he had asked. And if not, then he would teach, or find some way to support them. But his deepest wish was to be married to her, to know that they would always be together.

Desmond. He answered to the most yearn-ing, deeply felt part of herself.

Tomorrow afternoon she would see him again. He had planned a stroll through the park, and then dinner.

Edith's heart swelled in anticipation. She lifted her rose-scented wrist to her nose and inhaled, remembering the tender embrace of just a few hours ago. And with that image filling her mind, she gave in to the sweet blanketing of sleep.

Chapter 5

❧

Mr. Rockwell droned on in the staff meeting on Monday morning, Lillian only half hearing what he said. She glanced over at Izzy and caught her trying to stifle a big yawn as she took the minutes. Rockwell usually didn't attend the Art Department meetings, but he wanted to apply some pressure in order to step up production time. She heard him reminding them about the poster contest and the themes he was looking for.

Lillian sat at the far end of the table, tapping a pencil on her notebook, her mind on the weekend and what had gone wrong. The unexpected tension between Tommy and Charles. Between her and Charles. The coldness she had shown him on Saturday night after their disagreement about her job. Sometime during the night, she had placed her hand on his chest, with the intention to set everything aright on Sunday. She only vaguely remembered the phone ringing in the early hours. But when she awoke in the morning, it was to find Charles already dressed and preparing to leave. He had received a call from naval headquarters, requesting his immediate return. He kissed her goodbye, and quietly left, leaving an aching distance between them.

And now it would be over two weeks before she saw him – not until Christmas week. She wished they could start all over again and do it better this time.

Everything had been fine, at least between them, until their conversation about her job. She hadn't meant to snap at him, and wished she had simply explained how she felt. He would understand. She could have explained that she was at a point in her work as an artist that was important to her development. To quit her job now, with no guarantee of future work would be a setback. And what if –

"And the same goes for you artists," Rockwell continued, looking directly at her.

Lillian looked up. What had he been saying?

He leaned forward and frowned. "I understand that we're still waiting on submissions for the poster contest. The deadline is coming up. What are you all waiting for?" He scowled at the list of names handed to him by the head of Art, and began reading them off.

"Mr. Gilford. What's your excuse?"

"I just submitted it before the meeting, Mr. Rockwell. A 'loose lips' theme. Silhouette of a sinking ship against a fiery sky."

Rockwell grunted his approval. "Miss Albrecht? Can you deliver on another Army Air Forces poster?"

"Yes, sir. Nearly finished, sir. Handsome pilot. Lots of planes. Pretty girls in the background," she said, fluttering her fingers in the air.

"Mrs. Drooms?"

Lillian sat up straight. "Well – I'm considering a couple of different ideas. The Nurse Cadet Program and a War Bonds theme – "

"Too tame. Save those for the weeklies. We need to stir up sentiment – and not the sappy kind." He shuffled through a pile of drawings on the table, and glanced up at her. "Understood?"

Lillian dipped her head in agreement.

"And speaking of the weeklies," he continued to address her, "how's that cover coming along – the one with the dame on the ladder decorating a Christmas tree?"

The head of Art leaned over to Rockwell and whispered, "She's taking the decorations *off* the tree, actually, sir. For the New Year's *insert*, actually." He noticed Rockwell's displeasure at being corrected and quickly added, "But that deadline is indeed fast approaching." He swept his hand to Lillian to respond.

Rockwell was now glaring at Lillian. "Well?"

Lillian folded her hands on the table, hoping to give the impression of a well-thought-out response. "Yes. Well, sir, that image has already been done a few times, so I was thinking – "

"I don't pay you to think, Mrs. Drooms, I pay you to draw, and if I ask for a dame on a ladder, then you'll give me a dame on a ladder! It sells magazines and that's what we're in the business of doing." He pushed the drawings aside. "Make it your own, if you have to – sweet. But make it patriotic and alluring. And I want her in a dress. None of this menswear business."

Lillian cringed. There it was again. *Sweet, soft, tame* – words used to describe her drawings of family, gardens, children.

Rockwell pushed back his chair, and addressed everyone with a final remark. "And I don't have to remind you of WPB restrictions on garments – no cuffs, no pleats, no excesses of any kind." He leaned in the direction of Lillian. "Less fabric in general, if you catch my drift," he said, raising his eyebrows at her.

Only Izzy noticed the slight pursing of Lillian's lips at his unsubtle remark.

"Meeting adjourned," he snapped, with all the authority of having slammed a gavel on the table.

A few employees flocked around Rockwell as he left the room. Izzy walked up to Lillian, who remained seated, and leaned against the table.

"Another dame on a ladder," said Lillian.

Izzy smiled and shrugged. "That's what you get for making her so fetching the first time."

"Patriotic and alluring." Lillian groaned and pushed herself away from the table. "I'll dress her in a red, white, and blue negligee – short. Do you think that will make him happy?"

"Only if it's see-through. We on for lunch?"

"Yes," laughed Lillian, walking with Izzy to the elevator. "Sometimes I feel that I'm losing any artistic vision I might have had, drawing to specification as I am."

"Well," said Izzy, "of course you have to fulfill your assignments, but you have to stay true to yourself."

Exactly what Lillian had always believed, and she tried to live in accordance with that idea – but this was work. This was different. "I have to give him what he asks for."

"That's just it," Izzy countered. "He doesn't know what he wants until he sees it. You're the artist. *That's* what he's paying you for. I say go with your instincts."

Lillian considered this – and quickly realized that she lacked that kind of confidence. Perhaps at some later date, she thought, when she had proven herself, when others saw her as an artist.

The elevator opened and Izzy stepped in. "I'll meet you in the lobby."

*

On their way to the little café around the corner, Izzy kept snatching glances at Lillian. "You look a bit down in the mouth. You're not letting Rockwell get to you, are you?"

"Hmm? Oh, no," she answered.

"Already missing Charles, is that it?"

"No. I mean yes, I do miss him, but – The weekend didn't go at all well."

"No?" asked Izzy, taking her arm companionably. "Why not? Did you have the dinner for Gino?"

"Oh, that was the high point," said Lillian. "We had a wonderful time. But then – I don't know. It seemed like everyone was on edge. Tommy behaved rudely to Charles. He seems to resent the fact that Charles is away – and I know it made Charles feel bad. Then Charles and I quarreled about – stupid things. Little things. He hinted that I should quit my job. Somehow it set me off. I know he's just worried, but he doesn't realize how hard it was for me to get this job. What it means to me."

"Maybe you need to tell him."

"I did. Sort of. I just can't see myself sitting at home. I guess I'm afraid that I might just sit there and worry and not get anything done."

"I know what you mean. I'd go bonkers if I had to stay home. I need to keep busy." Izzy pulled open the door to the cafe. "Gosh, are we later than usual?"

The place was crowded and they had to wait for several minutes. They finally settled for a seat at the counter and put in their order for sandwiches while the overwhelmed waitress filled their coffee cups.

Lillian continued with her train of thought as she poured in some milk. "It would serve no purpose right now. If there was some reason why I had to be at home anyway, then it would make some sense. I would enjoy being at home."

Izzy studied Lillian's expression. "You mean if there was a baby? Is that what's bothering you?"

Lillian lifted one shoulder in a thwarted shrug. "I don't know. I guess I was hoping it would happen."

Izzy rubbed Lillian's arm. "Well, it can take time, and that's the one thing you two haven't had. You married in January and then he was called up in – what was it, March?"

"February 20th. And we've only had a few scattered weekends together since then."

"Well, there you have it."

A fleeting sadness passed over Lillian's face; for a few brief seconds she saw a baby in her arms, Charles smiling down at them. And then the vision was yanked away from her. "No. I think maybe I'm too old. I'm thirty-seven now." She took a sip of coffee. "How about you, Izzy? Isn't that something you want out of life?"

"Oh, if the right guy comes along," Izzy said breezily. "But I'm not going to lose any sleep over it, that's for sure. I'm too busy enjoying my life. There's a dance tonight to raise funds for the USO, and I intend to raise some serious bucks."

The waitress soon set their sandwiches down in front of them and then hurried back through the swinging doors to the kitchen.

Izzy lifted her sandwich, took a big bite, and gave a sigh of pleasure. Then she moved her shoulders back and forth to the swing music on the radio.

Lillian put an elbow on the counter and watched Izzy. "Such gusto. And on a Monday." She took the toothpick out of her sandwich. "I don't know where you get all your energy."

"Didn't you notice? I took a little nap during the meeting. You're going to have to tell me what Rockwell said so I can write up the minutes."

"No, seriously – you're out volunteering at least three nights a week, you have an active social life, a full-time job – and yet you're always bursting with energy. Don't you ever slow down?"

Izzy leaned her head back and laughed. "No time for it! There's too much to do – there's money to be made, dances to be danced, soldiers that need an ear, or in some cases a kiss. I gotta keep moving. I'll slow down once this war is over."

Izzy took another bite of her sandwich and talked with a half-full mouth. "I love my work at the Stage Door. You should see the look on those kids' faces. Oh my God, Private Taylor, on Friday – no, it was Saturday – what a sweetheart!" She set her sandwich down, and for a moment was back at the Canteen. She sighed, and then picked up her sandwich again. "Some of them want me to be their best girl and want to write to me. I must have a dozen boys I'll be writing to. Others are fresh and want to flirt. But most just want to talk about home, their girls, their families."

Lillian briefly imagined such a scene. "Such young boys. It sounds heartbreaking."

"No. It isn't," said Izzy, brushing crumbs from her hands, "because none of us will let it be. We all put on a brave face. Those boys are determined to come back home. Soon. And I tell them all they better, because Izzy Briggs will be waiting for them."

"But don't you ever get tired – just physically tired?"

"Sore feet some nights." Izzy turned to Lillian, as if she just realized something. "But I have to say, I've never slept better! I think all the girls feel the same way. It's exciting, and every night is different."

Lillian lifted her sandwich, about to take another bite, when she remembered what Charles had said about Edith. "By the way, you were right about Edith. Charles asked Mr. Mason, and apparently Edith is seeing someone – an actor."

Izzy nodded. "Desmond Burke. He's a Shakespearean actor, and he's done a lot of off-Broadway. He seems like a swell guy. Sure helps out at the Canteen. Several girls have set their caps at him, but he wasn't interested. Until Edith-the-mystery-woman showed up. He can't keep his eyes off her." Izzy took another bite of her sandwich, and then cocked her head as she considered something. "She's a funny mix."

"Edith? I know what you mean. I was trying to explain it to Charles. She's both earthy and other-worldly at the same time. That contrast is part of what makes her so beautiful. That low, soft voice, and her sudden actions. I told Charles that she has the kind of beauty an artist would appreciate."

"You're right. She's full of contradictions. At first, I thought maybe she was shy. The way she sometimes looks down or away – but then other times her gaze is piercing, goes right through you. She's different – I like her. It's almost like she's from another time. She dresses in clothes a good decade old, sometimes older – longer hems, scarves and shawls. I assumed it was to disguise her limp – though it's really not so noticeable. But those older fashions somehow suit her." Izzy picked up the dessert menu. "Feel like some ice cream? While we can still get it?"

"Sure, why not? Chocolate for me," Lillian said to the waitress.

"And I'll have peppermint. Two scoops. With chocolate syrup," Izzy called out to the vanishing waitress.

"Anyway," said Lillian. "I'm happy for Edith that she has a friend."

"Oh, I think he's more than a friend. I saw them by chance late one night – early morning really – getting into a cab. And they didn't look like friends."

Lillian considered this, holding her coffee cup. "I guess that's why Mr. Mason is concerned. Well, she's a grown woman, after all." She took a sip of her coffee, and suddenly looked over at Izzy. "And what were *you* doing out so late?"

"I'm a grown woman, too," laughed Izzy.

"Isabell Briggs! Are you seeing someone? And you didn't tell me?"

"Well, not exactly. I saw someone once or twice. Once, actually. He only had a 24-hour leave. Staff Sergeant Parker." Izzy let out a moan of pleasure. "Gorgeous." She shook off the memory. "I'm sure I'll never see him again. Whichever shore he lands on, the girls are sure to swoon over him."

"Izzy!" Lillian leaned over and whispered, "Do you mean – you spent the night with him? At a hotel?"

"We were lucky to find one, let me tell you. Everything is overbooked these days." She shook her head at some thought. "Dating the GIs from the Canteen is strictly prohibited. They'll take away our IDs if we get caught. What a crazy rule," she said, rolling her eyes. "Here are these young men, going away, very likely to die. And we're supposed to shake their hands and say 'good luck soldier?'" She shook her head at the impossibility, and made way for the ice cream that was just being placed in front of her.

Lillian was still staring open-mouthed at her friend. She picked up a spoon and looked down at her ice cream, briefly imagining Izzy and her clandestine encounter: hat pulled low over one eye, coat collar turned up, stepping out of a shadowy doorway, into the arms of a handsome young man. All very romantic. But, still.

Though she was only a few years older than Izzy, Lillian took on the tone of an older sister. "Well, I hope at least you were careful."

"Oh, I'm *always* careful." Izzy smiled with a wink, and dug into her ice cream.

Chapter 6

❧

Tommy and Gabriel left school with their salvage drive partners, the Kinney brothers, who lived down the street from them. Mickey, Tommy's age, was the team captain. Though his younger brother, Billy, only sporadically helped out with the drive, Gabriel always enjoyed it more when he was around.

"We gotta come up with something that will make people want to give us their scrap metal and paper," said Tommy. "Everybody has junk just lying around. Stuff they don't need."

"We just need a better plan," said Mickey. "Knocking on doors with our bags held out isn't working."

"It works for Halloween," said Billy.

"Well, this is different." Tommy kicked at some dirty snow edging the sidewalk. "All we got last week was a total of sixteen tin cans, some newspapers, and an old toaster. We'll never win the prize that way. We only have two more weeks before Christmas."

"Maybe you need to explain how important it is," offered Billy.

Tommy threw his arms up. "I keep telling everyone that one old shovel can be used to make four grenades. But it doesn't seem to make a difference."

Billy made explosion sounds and covered his head with his arms as he ducked for cover.

Gabriel enjoyed the dramatic enactment, but then he suddenly turned to Tommy. "Maybe people don't want to think about grenades at Christmastime."

"You got a point there," said Mickey. "Well, we gotta think of something. And fast."

They walked in silence for a few moments, except for Billy, who was now walking with one foot on the curb, the other on the street. "Look!" he cried, hobbling up and down. "I'm a wounded soldier!"

"Hey!" said Gabriel, stopping. "How about we sing Christmas carols?"

Billy started to sing, "Good King Wenceslas looked out," still bobbing up and down.

"Not now," laughed Gabriel. "I mean for our drive."

Tommy shook his head. "Don't be a dope, Gabe."

Mickey grabbed Tommy's arm. "Wait a second!" He ran a scenario in his mind and then cried out, "That's brilliant! Don't you see? It'll put everyone in the holiday spirit. They'll all want to give. I can see it now. We'll have more scraps than we can carry."

"Oh, bring us your scrappy papers," sang Billy.

"Oh, bring us your flattened tin cans," added Mickey.

"Oh, bring us your scrappy metals, and bring them right now!" sang Gabriel, finishing up with a fisted flourish.

Tommy finally joined in, throwing his arm around Mickey. "We *won't* go until we get some, we *won't* go until we get some…"

By the time they got to Mrs. Kuntzman's brownstone, they had run through several carols, and were bursting with confidence that their plan would work.

"We're gonna nail this contest!" hollered Tommy. "See you guys tomorrow!" He started to run up the stairs, as Mickey and Billy raced each other home.

"You sure are in a hurry for a babysitter you don't want to go to," said Gabriel, trailing behind. "Hey, look! Here comes Amy."

Tommy froze on the top step as Amy approached.

"Hi, Amy!" Gabriel called out.

Amy was walking alone, carrying her books. She gave a big wave. "Hiya, Gabriel. Hello, Tommy. What are you guys up to?"

"Oh, hi," said Tommy, as if he just now saw her.

Gabriel pointed up to the brownstone. "This is where our babysitter –"

"We're going to ask someone here for some scrap metal," said Tommy, cutting him off. "For the salvage drive."

Amy stood in front of the steps and smiled up at Tommy. "Are you collecting a lot of stuff?"

"Uh, not really," said Tommy.

Amy waited for Tommy to elaborate but he suddenly became fixated on his shoe.

"Skippy Petrie stopped by our house to ask for tins and paper but I told him I was saving all our scraps for you. I mean for your team."

Tommy looked up, not sure if he had heard her correctly.

"Gee, thanks, Amy," Gabriel said. He knew he was supposed to let Tommy do all the talking, but for some reason Tommy wasn't saying anything.

Amy smiled over at Gabriel, then back to Tommy. "He even asked for rubber, and that drive doesn't start until January. He's trying to get a head start. No fair! My mom knows to save everything for you, just in case he comes back."

Tommy cracked his knuckles wondering if he would have to knock at her door to collect the things. What if her mother answered? Or her father?

"Have you decided on your science project?" Amy asked, as she pushed her glasses up her nose.

"Not yet." Tommy swallowed, and searched around for the next words. "Have you?"

"I'm thinking of doing something on botany. Or the planets." After each topic, she waited for Tommy's reaction. "Or maybe cloud formation. Do you think that's interesting?"

"Yeah, sure." Tommy gave a quick look at the overcast sky but didn't see a single cloud to comment on.

"The teacher said we could form teams." Amy twisted from side to side, offering up suggestions one at a time as she waited for Tommy's response. "If we wanted to. Sometimes it's easier that way. You know – two minds are better than one."

Gabriel opened his eyes wide and smiled. Here was Tommy's big chance. Easy as pie.

"Yeah. Well, see ya," said Tommy, and he ran up the stairs.

"Oh. Okay. Bye," said Amy. She gave a light shrug, and began to walk away.

"Bye, Amy!" cried Gabriel, following Tommy up the stairs.

Inside the vestibule, Gabriel poked Tommy in the side. "What happened to 'Be bold?'"

"I was. I talked to her, didn't I?"

"Not like Gino said to."

Mrs. Kuntzman opened her door. "Come, come boys. Inside. I make youse some Ovaltine and oatmeal raisin cookies. How about that?"

"Sounds great!" Tommy said, whipping off his coat, and suddenly interested in the snack.

Gabriel gave him another poke. "You should have said you liked clouds and would be her science partner."

Tommy frowned. "I'll – I'll talk to her more next time," he said in a low voice. "You have to take it a step at a time."

Gabriel shook his head at Tommy, who had already run into the kitchen.

*

Lillian wiped the steam from the mirror, and breathed a sigh of relaxation after her bath. She searched inside the basket on the shelf, then inside the medicine cabinet. She wanted to put a few pin curls in place, but she couldn't find a single hair pin. She opened the bathroom cupboard, and lifted the folded towels. She hadn't noticed that she was running low. How could she have possibly lost them all?

Her attention was diverted by the sounds of Tommy and Gabriel arguing. She tied her robe, and went out to the kitchen.

"It's *my* lunchbox!" cried Gabriel.

"But we need it for the drive! It's on the list of items to collect."

"But it's still good. You don't have to give away *good* things. That's why it's called a *scrap* drive!"

"Gabriel," said Tommy, dramatically placing his hand on Gabriel's Hopalong Cassidy lunchbox. "This could be the bullet that kills Hitler."

"I don't want my lunchbox to be a bullet. Use your own!"

"I am, but we need – "

"Boys, what's going on?"

Gabriel snatched the lunchbox and held it tightly under his arm.

"We need things for our salvage drive, but Gabriel won't give me his lunchbox. They have plenty of those new ones made out of cardboard. That's what we're supposed to be using."

Lillian looked in the bag that Tommy had on the kitchen table. She saw two flattened tin cans, and at the bottom of the bag – "My hairpins! Thomas Drooms! You can't just take things from people without asking! I just spent ten minutes looking for these," she said, gathering up her hair pins. "And that's Gabriel's lunchbox. You can give yours if you want to, but leave Gabriel's alone." She took a good look at Tommy. "What's gotten into you lately, anyway?"

Tommy plopped down on the chair. "Nothing! I just want to do a good job on the scrap drive. And so far, it's just one big snafu after another. People say they already gave their scraps to someone else, or brought them to the store when they dropped off their grease. Billy keeps quitting on us. So far we're in fourth place, and – "

"But there's a right way and a wrong way to go about it," Lillian said, wondering at Tommy's increasing frustration with everything.

"Hey," said Gabriel, "what does snafu mean? Gino forgot to tell me."

"Each letter stands for a word," Tommy explained. "Situation normal, all f– "

"Tommy!" snapped Lillian, before he could finish the offending word.

"All fouled up," said Tommy with a mischievous glint in his eye.

"Oh. So we'll get rid of all the snafus, and try out our plan," said Gabriel.

"We only have two more weeks left," said Tommy.

Lillian tweaked his nose and then put her arm around him. "Anything you collect will help the war effort. That's the main thing. Besides, a lot can happen in two weeks."

"Yeah, I know," said Tommy. He lifted his face to her. "Sorry about the hairpins, Mom."

Lillian coiled a strand of hair and secured it with a hair pin. "I saw Mrs. Wilson today, and she said she's going to clean out her closets and tell everyone else in her building to do the same thing. Maybe that will help."

"Mommy, can we have hot water bottles tonight?" asked Gabriel.

Lillian put in a few more pin curls. "You boys get ready for bed, and I'll start boiling some water."

"They're collecting hot water bottles, too," said Tommy.

Lillian's hand froze in the last pin curl.

"There's a rubber shortage," he said. "Bad."

Lillian dropped her hands and considered giving up the water bottles. But with the fuel rationed, the apartment was often cold. I have to keep my children warm, she thought. But what about the men in faraway places, suffering, dying, to protect us? Everything should go to help them.

"It's okay, Mom," said Tommy. "We don't start the rubber drive until after Christmas."

Lillian put a hand on Tommy's shoulder. "Tomorrow we'll look down in the basement. Make sure there's nothing we're forgetting. Gabriel's tricycle is down there. We won't be needing that anymore. Maybe there are some other things. Our old gardening tools are down there."

"No. We need those for our Victory Garden this summer," said Gabriel. "On the roof. Mrs. Wilson said there's going to be a garden on every roof on our block."

Lillian let out a deep sigh. "We'll sort it all out tomorrow. For now, I want you to take your baths."

"Sure, Mom." Tommy eyed Gabriel's lunchbox and began to hum, 'We Wish You a Merry Christmas.'"

Gabriel clutched his lunchbox.

"Go on, Tommy," said Lillian. "You first."

"Okay, okay," said Tommy, heading for the bathroom.

She took the lunchbox and set it on the counter.

"Mommy," said Gabriel, "we're lucky we live on the third floor."

"Why is that?" asked Lillian, filling a pan of water and then setting it on the stove.

"Because if we're gassed, we'll be above it."

Lillian turned to him. What on earth was he talking about?

"Today we learned what to do in a gas attack. They said to go to the highest spot in your house because gas is heavy and will sink."

Lillian stared at Gabriel. Was her little boy really thinking about what to do in a gas attack?

"Don't worry, Mom," said Gabriel, seeing her frightened expression. "If it comes up this high, we'll go up on the roof."

She gave him a quick hug, and tried to sound cheerful. "I don't think we'll have to worry about that. Why don't you finish reading *The Long Winter*, and then you can tell me how it ends."

Gabriel was immediately back in the 1880s, the Dakota Territory blizzards blowing hard. He pinched his eyebrows together in concern. "The trains have stopped running, and Pa's gettin' worried. They have to twist the hay into ropes for fuel, so they can keep the ole stove going," he said, his hands torqueing the imaginary hay.

Lillian shivered dramatically and lit the burner. "Thank goodness we have hot water bottles."

Gabriel laughed, and ran off to get ready for bed.

Once the boys were tucked in with their books and hot water bottles, Lillian sat on the couch and stared into the empty fireplace. She tucked her legs under her and wondered where they were all heading in this war, and hoped that Tommy and Gabriel would never have to experience the battlefield. She kept thinking of that poor mother who had lost all five of her sons last month. All on the same ship in the Pacific. How does one go on after that?

She tried to keep focused on the day to day, to make sure the boys felt as safe and secure as possible. But every now and then, she was flooded by a sickening sense of dread. And fear. Ever since that *Life* magazine article came out last year. As she remembered the photographs that had been smuggled out of Poland, her face crumpled in pity and revulsion at what was being done to those poor people. The emaciated bodies, the hopeless faces. That poor, pathetic child, more dead than alive – pencil-thin arms and legs, a horribly protruded stomach, dark hollow eyes that stared back at her, asking Why? Why? – an image that would haunt her forever. She closed her eyes as she remembered the horrors that had been written about. No one could have imagined it could be that bad. And now more stories were trickling in from the Pacific about an incident that occurred in the spring from some place called Bataan.

Before the magazine article, Lillian had believed that such stories were propaganda and exaggerations. She could not accept that such horrors were true, that human beings were capable of such atrocities. She knew that war was terrible, and that some people behaved like monsters – but that so many people willingly participated in such acts, or turned their heads – she still wanted to believe that it couldn't be true. But that was no longer possible. She had to admit to an ugliness in human nature that she never before believed in.

She tried to quell the mounting despair, tried to put aside the disturbing images, and focus on today. What could she do now? Action. That was always her remedy against despair.

Her sketch pad sat on the corner of the coffee table, reminding her of her work assignment. She would have to submit something for the contest – might as well get started.

The images that came to her were not the ones that Rockwell was asking for. She wanted to counter the horrors of war. She wanted to draw mothers packing up boxes to send to their sons, volunteers on the home front helping where they could, children pulling a wagon for their scrap drive.

She didn't want to draw caricatures of the enemy. Or fields of barbed wire, and sinking ships. And yet she had to submit something. And prove that she could draw something that wasn't *sweet*. She groaned at Rockwell's assessment of her work.

She lifted her pencil and sketched a soldier holding a tattered flag in battle. Then scratched it out. A proud father watching his son leave home. She crumbled the paper. Then she tried a train station, with a couple saying goodbye to each other. A good composition, but it was still too sweet. She erased the male figure, and let her pencil make a few lines, and a few more, drawing the man as a skeleton. He still wore his officer's cap, and the couple clung to each other in a passionate farewell. She picked up a blue oil pastel crayon and shaded the woman's coat, the officer's cap.

Leaning back, she held the drawing out at arm's length, expecting to be pleased with the result. But with a gasp, she covered her mouth, realizing that the couple looked like her and Charles. Appalled, she ripped out the drawing and tore it up. What was she thinking! A horrible sense of foreboding filled her. She got up and threw the bits of paper into the fireplace and struck a match. The paper caught fire and then shriveled to black.

She held her face in her hands. How had the world become such a horrible place? The war's darkness was enveloping the world, her world, her mind. She stood looking into the empty fireplace, the ashy grate expanding into an ever-widening black void.

Then came the light, clear voice of Gabriel – halting the downward pull of despair. "Goodnight, Mommy!" he called out, as he often did before going to sleep.

Those beautiful, pure words of childhood pierced her and filled her with gratitude that here was a tiny space still untouched by the horrors of war. Gratitude that her children were safe, well-fed, and ignorant of the awfulness of human nature.

She went to their room and gazed down at her boys. Tommy was already asleep, with the lamplight shining on his sweet face. She picked up his comic book that had fallen to the floor. Gabriel was lying on his side smiling up at her, his hands tucked under his cheek, just like a little storybook boy.

"I didn't get to the end of my book, Mom, but Pa says the spring thaw is finally coming, and the train will get through. Everything's going to be okay."

"Thank goodness!" she said, putting her hand on his cheek.

She kissed them both goodnight, and turned off the light.

Then she finally went to bed, feeling that she had been rescued.

Chapter 7

⁓

Mason looked up from his book as his wife placed a steaming cup of coffee next to him. Just as she turned away, he playfully reached for her hand and gave it a quick kiss. He took a sip of coffee, and sank deeper into his old wing-backed chair. A small lift of contentment formed on his lips as he glanced around the living room. It was late afternoon, and though snowflakes drifted past the window, inside it was snug, comfortable. Light from the lamp behind his chair filled the room with a sense of warmth and hominess. A faint scent of pine came from the small Christmas tree in the corner. The radiator softly hissed. The workweek was over, and he was surrounded by his family – his favorite way to spend the day.

Susan had put the baby down for a nap, made the coffee, and now, with a sigh of pleasure at having a little time to relax, she plumped down in the chair across from him, and enjoyed a few sips of coffee. As she gathered up her knitting, their five-year-old daughter climbed onto her lap with her doll. Susan managed to knit with the little girl snuggled up next to her.

The eleven-year-old twins sat in the window seat facing each other, engrossed in their books. A deep-green afghan was draped over their bent knees, forming a small mountain between them.

Mason was indulging in his Christmas tradition of reading Charles Dickens. Every December he decided on a book by his favorite author. Last year he had chosen *Bleak House* – this year he was re-reading *Nicholas Nickleby*. He was just settling into his book when his domestic bliss was abruptly interrupted by the whirlwind of his mother and his youngest sister, Alice, as they burst into the room.

"We're off!" cried his mother, checking the contents of her purse before snapping it shut. "We must hurry before the stores close. We're on a hunt for red satin for the girls' costumes."

Mason set his book down, with a touch of annoyance. "I thought you were finished with all that *Fractured Follies* business," he said.

"That was for the drama last weekend," explained Alice. "Now we're working on costumes for the chorus line," and with that she gave a high kick.

"Bravo, Alice," applauded his mother, "but do be careful of the lampshade."

Alice straightened the shade, and sat on the edge of the couch. "I wish you'd join us, Robert. We have far too many women dressed as men. Sort of Shakespeare in reverse. Won't you reconsider?"

"You'll not find *me* in any theatricals. There's enough of that going on in this house as it is." He gave a look over his glasses at Edith, who was just coming down the stairs, dressed to go out.

"We've been such a success," continued Alice, "that they've lined us up at three more veterans' hospitals. The men are wild about us! The patients, I mean. And these chorus line costumes will be stunning!" Alice pulled on her coat and followed her mother out the door, calling back, "But don't worry, Robert, we won't spend too much."

"It's not the cost I'm worried about!" he shouted after them. "It's that I never know where anyone is anymore!" He stared at the closed door in exasperation.

Edith perched on the hall tree bench, pulling on her boots, mildly amused by her brother's ongoing frustration with the family.

Mason rose from his chair and paced the living room, looking from Susan to Edith. "Claudia wanting to join the WAVES, Alice and Helen in chorus lines and doing God knows what."

Susan was accustomed to her husband's periodic bursts of vexation with his sisters. She shifted her little girl to the other side of her lap, and then calmly resumed her knitting. "Times are changing, Robert. The girls are merely keeping up with them. They all want to do their duty."

"And have as much fun as possible in the process," he added.

"Well, what's wrong with that, for heaven's sake? We need to counteract the dreadful news somehow. I'm glad for their cheerfulness. And it helps to dispel some of *your* gloom." Susan exchanged a smiling glance with Edith.

"And you, Edith!" Mason called into the hallway. "They're taking their cue from you – out at all hours, running around with an actor!"

Edith stood in front of the hall mirror and positioned her hat. "Berate me all you want, if it makes you feel better, but don't you dare disparage a man that you haven't even had the simple courtesy to meet."

Mason plopped down in his chair, threw his hands up, and let them drop heavily on his lap. "I just don't understand it, Edith. Why now? Why him? When you had other chances with stable, dependable young men – "

"Like Jack?" Edith shot a cutting glance at her brother. But the shadow that passed over his face made her regret her response.

She crossed into the living room and placed a hand on the back of his chair. "You fret too much, Robert. A useless way to spend your time. We're all old enough to be making our own decisions. For God's sake, I'm almost thirty-four. This could be my last chance for happiness. You should rejoice. No one wants a maiden sister hanging about forever."

Mason's head snapped up and his face filled with worry. Perhaps the relationship had progressed further than he thought. He raised his palms, as if bracing against the onslaught of change. "Just – don't do anything rash. Promise me that much, Edith. Everything is so – volatile right now." He rubbed his brow. "No one is thinking clearly."

"Including you, dear brother."

For the first time, Edith noticed the gray starting in at his temples, and the weariness behind his eyes. Her heart went out to him. "Don't worry so much, Robert," she said in a kinder tone.

"Promise me, Edith," he asked again, looking up at her.

"I can't start making promises. But think about it. Have you ever known me to be rash? Ever?"

"Headstrong," he responded, unwilling to concede that she was right.

She gave a light laugh in agreement. "That's different." Then she kneeled down beside him and placed her hand on the armrest. "Won't you meet him, Robert? I'm sure you would like him."

Mason took a deep breath, fixed his eyes on the carpet, and remained silent.

Edith stood, closing up once again. "Very well," she said, pulling on her gloves. "I won't ask you again." She looped her lacy white scarf around her neck, raised her eyebrows at Susan, as if in comment on his stubbornness, and left the house.

Mason glanced over at his wife, expecting a mild reprimand.

But Susan merely eyed him over her knitting. "Perhaps you should join the girls," she remarked playfully. "At least that way you would know where they are. Two of them, anyway."

"No, thank you," he said, reaching for the newspaper. There was no way he could enjoy his book now. "I'm surprised they haven't tried to corral you." He gave the newspaper a firm shake.

"Oh, they have. There's a can-can number they think I would be right for."

Aghast, Mason lowered the paper with his mouth open. Then catching the merriment in his wife's eyes, he quickly raised the newspaper to hide the foolish smile that crept about his mouth. He had actually believed her.

They sat quietly for a few moments, Mason apparently engrossed in his newspaper, Susan closely observing him now and then. She smiled as her little girl sang a lullaby and rocked her doll to sleep.

She knew exactly what was bothering her husband. Better to address it than to dance all around it. "They won't take you, anyway, Robert," she said softly.

Mason turned to the opposite page, folded it back, and punched the newspaper into place. "I told you. No stages for me."

"I'm not talking about the *Fractured Follies*, as you well know." She knitted another row, and watched him lower the paper with an air of defeat, all the little lines of worry around his eyes deepening.

She set her knitting down, and her eyes filled with tenderness. "You might get around the fact of your age and your family status. But that wheezy chest of yours would never pass inspection. You might as well accept it."

Mason frowned at the memory of this time last year, when he had tried to enlist – and was summarily rejected. Unfit. A fresh wave of shame washed over him. He set the newspaper aside. "It just feels wrong. I'm as fit as any man." He stood and began pacing again. "All these young boys going off to fight. And some older ones, as well. Many of them fought in the Great War, and here they are fighting again. Risking their lives for a second time. Look at Mr. Drooms."

"You can't compare yourself to him. For one thing, he was single when he enlisted. And his experience in the North Atlantic is invaluable. You said so yourself." She could see that her words had little effect. "And he couldn't do it without you here to run the business. You know that."

Mason scooped up his little girl from Susan's lap, and lifted her up to the ceiling, enjoying her cries of delight.

He set her down and she raised her arms. "Again! Again!"

Mason picked her up and walked around the room with her, lifting her high now and then, and smiling at her giggles. "I know I'm one of the lucky ones. Not to have to leave my children. Or you." He stood next to Susan, and bent down to kiss her forehead. "But it's not right."

*

Edith linked her arm with Desmond's as they walked through the forest-like Ramble in Central Park, the dirt path lightly covered with snow. Every now and then Desmond helped her to step over a fallen branch, or held back a bramble to allow her to pass.

"Are you sure you're all right?" he asked, taking Edith's arm as they climbed a few wide steps hewn from rock. "This isn't too much for you?"

Edith gave a small smile at his concern. "I told you, I'm strong!"

After a few more steps, she realized that her slenderness, not to mention her limp, was at odds with her words. "Well, stronger than I look, anyway." She squeezed his arm, appreciative of his considerate nature.

She had been following him, letting him lead the way through the woods, when suddenly, through the bare trees, she caught a glimpse of the pale gray tower, and recognized where they were headed.

"The Castle!" she cried, quickening her step as the stone structure rose up before them. "One of our first days together."

Desmond smiled at her enthusiasm, gratified that she held the memory as fondly as he did.

She climbed up the steps and let her eyes travel around the area, remembering the various scenes from Shakespeare that Desmond and his friends had performed. "Did you ever see the photographs and film clips?"

"Artie showed me just the other day. Hit and miss. But every image of you was absolutely breathtaking."

Edith gave him a doubtful look, but relished the memory. "I thought it great fun being part of your theatricals. Though I was glad when the sword fight was over."

"I was, too. I'm getting too old to be running up and down stairs, brandishing a sword."

"I couldn't bear to see you lying there, on the cold stone." She rested her eyes on the top of the steps where he had enacted the scene, and again her face took on a worried expression as she remembered his all too believable death.

"That anguish on your face is what prompted Artie to start clicking away at you. You were so shy. I don't know how he ever got you to agree to pose."

"I was pretending to be someone else, and so it was easy. You of all people should know that."

He took her arm and they climbed down the steps on the side of the courtyard, and then strolled over to the sloped Shakespeare Garden.

Edith smiled as they entered the garden, delighted at the snowy transformation. A stillness and hush had settled over it, with only a few small birds darting about the bare branches. The withered stalks of flowers and arched brambles were outlined in white; a few bright red berries clung to some of the bushes. She leaned her head back and breathed deeply, as if enjoying some subtle snow scent. "A winter garden," she said.

She glanced at the snow-covered bench, and, for a moment, Desmond worried that she was going to sit down on it. She often did the unexpected, and he was relieved that she apparently decided against it.

Instead she crossed over to the sundial and searched for a shadow, then raised her eyes to the gray and white dappled sky. A few small snowflakes softly landed on her hair, her shoulders.

Desmond observed the curve of her neck, her eyes cast heavenward. Something about her pierced his heart every time he gazed on her. He hoped she wouldn't shift her position – he wanted to drink in her beauty, impress it on his mind. He started to reach into his satchel, but she turned her head to scan the horizon.

Though her every move captivated him, she never stayed in one position for long. She was constantly gazing about, her mind engaged with her surroundings, her eyes registering delight, puzzlement, wonder – unless he happened to catch her when some impression resonated deep inside, and for a moment she would be utterly still, as she briefly left this world for another.

She returned her eyes to the sundial. "No shadow," she said, lifting her face to him. "Time has stopped for us."

He took her hands and held them to his chest. "Sometimes I think I might give it all up, the stage and all – and teach or something. Buy a little house for us somewhere. What would you say to that?"

Edith studied him, as she imagined the scenario he described. "I think you would miss it. The excitement of opening night, the lively cast parties, the intensity with which you study your lines."

They began to retrace their steps. "No," he said. "I think the only thing I would really miss is the becoming someone else. As you say." He stopped and faced her, placing his hands on her shoulders, allowing the castle to form a backdrop behind her. He beheld her face, so open, proud, and sensuous all at the same time. "A kiss," he said, bending down to her. "A kiss. My kingdom for a kiss."

She pressed her lips against his, and then laughed. "You see? You could never live without it. And you shouldn't."

"I don't know," he said, linking his arm with hers and continuing up the path. "Sometimes I think I would enjoy teaching Shakespeare to a bunch of young students. Open up the world of the bard to them, with all of its riches."

Edith wondered what he was getting at. "So why are we here, back at the Castle? You haven't told me why you brought me out in this cold, snowy weather."

"Because," said Desmond, reaching into his satchel and pulling out a camera, "I want to photograph you. I want my own pictures of you."

"All right. But I get to take some of you, as well."

For the next half hour they took turns posing, with Desmond reciting lines from various plays, and coaching Edith to take on expressions of Juliet, Titania, Ophelia – Edith surprising him once again with her ability to step into other worlds and effortlessly inhabit them.

They only stopped when the lighting grew dim.

Desmond returned his camera to his satchel and took Edith's arm. "And now – hie home! Where I shall prepare a feast for you, fit for the gods."

"Truly?" asked Edith, delighted by the prospect.

"Well, dinner, anyway," Desmond laughed.

"What are you going to make?"

"Pasta al pomodoro," he said, in an exaggerated Italian accent. "And antipasto, a loaf of fresh bread, and Chianti. We'll pick up something on our way home for dessert. And then we'll build a fire, and have dinner by candlelight."

*

Four hours later, Edith and Desmond sat in front of the dying fire. Desmond wrapped an old quilt, silky soft with many washings, around Edith's shoulders. He then poured out the last of the wine into their goblets.

Edith lifted her glass up to the fire, turning it to catch the glints of ruby in the etched vines.

Desmond watched her for a moment, then stood and reached for his satchel. He pulled out the camera and snapped a photo of Edith's upturned face in the soft lighting.

"Tell me, Desmond. Why all these photographs? Why now?"

It was a moment before he answered. "Because I want to take your image with me, wherever I go." He waited to see if Edith would ask the next question, but she merely waited for the words that would explain.

"You know I've signed up with the USO. Well, an actor from one of the camp show tours has fallen ill. And they need a Prospero, a sometimes stage manager, and – someone who could be gone for several months at a time."

Edith returned her gaze to the fire, seeing figures in the flames, reachings in the shadowy coals. She set her glass down, and pulled the blanket closer around her shoulders.

"I have to give them my answer by Monday." He sat down next to her and tried to interpret her expression. "I'm past the draft age. But I have to do what I can. It's little enough, with so many men dying, so many wounded. But if I can help to boost morale, give a laugh, offer some hope, then I must do it. You understand, don't you?"

"Of course, I do." Edith sat quietly, taking it all in. Then she impulsively took his hands and kissed them, and held them to her breast. "In all my thoughts of you, I never imagined that you would leave. When do you – "

"After Christmas. They have a temporary replacement through the holidays. Then I set sail the first of January."

"I see. Well then, you must. And I will be here when you return. Waiting for you." Again she kissed his hands.

"Edith, there's something else." He stood and reached up to the mantelpiece, and clasped something. Then he sat next to her and opened her hand, placing a ring in her palm. "I want us to be married. Before I go, I want us to be married."

Edith looked into his eyes, and then away. She held up the ring to the fire. A dark star-shaped stone, encircled with seed pearls. "It's beautiful."

"A garnet. It reminded me of you. It's from the 1880s or so."

He watched the soft flickering shadows on her face, her hair, her hands.

"Edith?"

She took a deep breath, and placed her hand on his arm. "Desmond, I want to marry you. But I think we should wait." His look of disappointment prompted her to explain. "In my heart, I am already your wife."

"Then why not make it official?"

"It wouldn't change anything that we already are. If you feel the same when you return, I'll marry you."

A shadow of sadness came over his eyes. "You doubt me, don't you? You think I might change?"

"No. I don't doubt you." Though in truth, she did. She didn't doubt that Desmond loved her. But that he could love her forever, she couldn't quite imagine. She had long ago given up the dream of being a happily married woman, and it proved a difficult dream to resurrect. Surely he would change his mind. Especially if he was going to be gone for months. Some beautiful actress would make him forget her.

"Is it because of your brother?"

Edith gratefully latched onto that excuse; it was much easier to blame her brother than her own insecurities. "I would like to give him time to get used to the idea. Poor Robert. He's been responsible for all of us for so long. Suddenly, it seems that we no longer need him." She gave a light laugh. "It's not easy being an older brother to us. At one time or another, we've all been a handful. We're a willful bunch. We get it from our mother." She remembered Robert rubbing his face, the weariness in his eyes. "He's had so much on his shoulders. I think it's quite aged him."

Desmond held her tight. "I was so sure you would say yes. But I want whatever is best for you. I will wait as long as you want."

"Let's wait until you return. See what the world has in store for us then."

"I can live with that," he said. "As long as you are truly my wife. Will you wear it, in the meantime? So that when I imagine you from wherever I'll be, I'll see the ring and know that you are mine?"

She slipped on the delicate garnet, and lifted her face to him. "I'll never take it off. It will become a part of me. Forever." Of that, she was sure. It would always be there to remind her of this moment. When the man she loved desired her as his wife. When the promise of the future surrounded her in sweetness.

Desmond jumped up. "Don't move. That's the photo I want. Just like that."

Edith's hair hung down in glossy waves about her shoulders, the quilt forming a kind of mantle.

"You look just like a queen. I could imagine that is ermine around your shoulders. It should be ermine." He took a few clicks. "Or a fairy princess. Yes. This is the image I want to take with me."

He wanted to capture that immediacy in her eyes, her gaze that both pierced and had a dreamy softness about it.

"My husband," was her only reply.

Chapter 8

◦⌇

"Where do all these people come from?" Lillian asked her neighbor Mrs. Wilson as they entered Mancetti's crowded grocery store.

"I think our neighborhood has doubled in size," said Mrs. Wilson. "And, of course, the ration coupons and lines slow everything down."

They heard snippets of conversations, all concerning the war. Mr. Mancetti was waving around a newspaper, denouncing Il Duce as a pompous fool, more concerned with his appearance than with the welfare of his people.

Others were discussing the recent North African invasion, with differing views. "With us in North Africa now," said one man, "it's just a matter of time before we lick 'em."

"Don't be so sure about that," countered an older man. "We're not prepared. Our artillery is old and inadequate. I hear the boys over there refer to our tanks as *Ronsons* – one piece of shrapnel and they blaze up like a cigarette lighter. They're no match for Hitler's panzers."

Others added their opinions, the conversation vacillating between bravado and doubt, confidence and cautious skepticism.

Tommy and Gabriel stopped in front of the comic book stand while Lillian and Mrs. Wilson went to the deli counter in the back. Lillian noticed yet another new young man behind the meat and cheese case. It seemed that just as she got used to one, he was called off to serve, and another filled the position. They were getting younger and younger.

Tommy suddenly felt Gabriel's elbow in his side and was about to yell at him, when Gabriel whispered, "Be bold!"

Tommy snapped to attention; there was Amy entering the store.

"Don't forget, you have to report back to Gino," Gabriel said.

Tommy stood immobile, eyes fixed on the *Superman* comic book in front of him. He swallowed, trying to think of the various stages of Gino's plan, but forgetting which point he was at – had he progressed to Point Two? And what was it? A present?

"Hi, Gabriel," said Amy. "Hi, Tommy." She gave a gasp of delight and reached for a *Captain*

Marvel comic book. "Oh, my gosh! You *have* to get this one, Tommy. It's *so* good. Billy Batson finds out that he has a *sister*! His long-lost twin Mary. And just like Billy, when she says 'Shazam!' she becomes amazingly strong and powerful and can do anything!" She handed the comic to Tommy to look at, and twisted her shoulders side to side. "But her powers come from the goddesses. Cause she's a girl."

Tommy unknotted a bit and studied the cover, nodding. "It sounds good. I think I'll get it."

"Read it and then tell me what you think," said Amy. "You should read it too, Gabriel."

"Okay. When Tommy's done with it, he can give it to me." Gabriel stared at Tommy, waiting for him to say something.

Afraid that Gabriel was going to elbow him again, Tommy turned to Amy. "How's your book drive going?"

"Not bad. We have about twenty books or so. At first it was kind of hard to ask people, but after a while it gets easy and they're happy to help out."

"Oh!" cried Gabriel. "I just remembered I have to tell Mom something. About my school lunch. Something bold." He widened his eyes at Tommy and left him on his own.

Tommy bit the inside of his mouth. "We might have some books at home to give away. I'll ask my mom."

"That'd be swell," said Amy, straightening her glasses. "We're collecting all kinds of books. Even comic books. The GIs like them. Isn't that funny? I didn't think they would, but my teacher said to be sure to include them, so I always ask and I *always* get some."

"I have lots I can give you," said Tommy, finally relaxing. "I don't really read them too much anymore. Just sometimes."

"I still read *Little Orphan Annie* all the time. I love it – and I took the Junior Commando Pledge, of course. But my all-time favorite story is *Anne of Green Gables*. That's a book. I'm on my fourth read. Have you read it?"

Amy was still filling Tommy in on the story's main characters, when Lillian and Gabriel walked up to them. Lillian tried to hide her surprise at seeing Tommy talking to a girl; he was usually so shy around them.

"Mom, I told Amy that we might have some books and comics to give away. Her team is collecting books."

"Hello, Amy," said Lillian, appreciating the girl's friendliness to Tommy. "I'm sure we have some books we can give you. I'll look around when I get back home."

Just then, a large, brisk woman walked up and greeted Lillian, offering her hand. "I'm Amy's mother, Mrs. Little."

Lillian took her hand and introduced herself.

The woman's smile broadened as she looked down at Tommy. "Oh, so *you're* Tommy! Amy can't stop talking about you. It's Tommy this, and Tommy that." She bent over slightly. "I understand you're going to be Amy's partner for the science project. She's *so* excited."

"Mom, I said he *might* be. I haven't even asked him yet." She cast her eyes back and forth from Tommy to Lillian to explain. "Our teacher said we could work in teams if we wanted."

"Well, that's a good idea," said Lillian. "Tommy can't decide on his topic. Maybe the two of you together can come up with something."

Mrs. Little smiled and winked at Tommy. "Amy was just saying that she wanted to go to the library today and get some ideas. I'd be happy if you would accompany her." She leaned into Lillian, adding, "I know it's close to home, but you just never know. Saboteurs coming ashore, U-boat's lurking off the coast. Goodness me!" She rolled her eyes to the ceiling.

"Can I, Mom?" asked Tommy. "We have to submit our idea before Christmas."

Lillian had to smile at his sudden, new-found enthusiasm. He still had plenty of time to decide.

"Of course, you can."

The two women made their purchases and left the store, Mrs. Little telling Lillian about their move from Ohio to Manhattan, and how difficult it had been to find an apartment to rent.

At the corner, Mrs. Little reached into her purse and tucked some coins into Amy's coat pocket. "And you can stop by the soda fountain on your way home, as long as you don't spoil your appetite. If that's all right with you, Mrs. Drooms."

When Lillian gave her assent, she saw Gabriel's face fill with disappointment at the idea of missing out on ice cream.

Amy smiled at Gabriel. "You can come, too, Gabriel. Maybe you can help us think of something. Three heads are better than two."

On first seeing Amy, Lillian had immediately taken to her, with her round glasses, brightly colored stockings, and girlish confidence. But that she had so readily included Gabriel in the outing, made Lillian like her all the more.

Gabriel looked up at Tommy with raised eyebrows, not sure if he would be helping or hindering.

Tommy threw his arm around Gabriel's shoulder. "Come on, Gabe. We'll be back in a couple of hours, Mom."

Lillian watched the three children head to the library, happy to see that Tommy was talking and grinning. Other than rolling the comic book around and around in his hands, he seemed perfectly at ease with Amy.

*

Lillian wasn't sure if it was the friendship with Amy or a few nights of successful salvage collecting that had boosted Tommy's morale, but she was glad to see him more like his old self, and more in the holiday spirit.

After lunch on Saturday, Tommy and Gabriel sat in the living room with Mickey and Billy, adding to their list of carols, and making sure they knew all the words. They had complained that Billy was humming too many of the words, or making them up as he went along.

As they practiced, Lillian had to stop now and then to listen. They all had nice voices, but Tommy's was particularly beautiful. The only time she had really heard him sing was while he was splashing in the bath tub, or singing along with his radio shows. But now, as she listened to him, she was struck by the beauty of his voice – it had an easy range, and a smooth tone. She pretended to be making a grocery list at the kitchen table as she listened to them rehearse.

Gabriel and Billy were feeling the presents under the tree and trying to guess what they might be, while Mickey wrote down the songs in the order they would be sung.

"We might as well do the same songs when we start on a new block," said Mickey. "All we really need are about seven songs or so. We'll finish with 'We Wish You a Merry Christmas' – with our salvage drive words, of course. We need one more. Any ideas?"

"How about that new one?" suggested Tommy – "'White Christmas.' They say all the servicemen are listening to it, wherever they are."

"Good thinking, Tommy!" said Mickey. "That'll tie in with our drive."

They began singing the song, hamming it up at the end.

"And it's short," said Mickey. "Come on, guys. We need to get going."

They slung their gunny sacks over their shoulders, looking like four little Santas in training, and hurried out the door.

"Back before 6:00, Tommy!" Lillian called after them. "I want you here for dinner."

"I know, I know," he called from one flight down.

Lillian watched them from the kitchen window. In spite of the war and all the bad news that daily filled the newspapers, she was beginning to feel that their first Christmas together as a family was going to be a good one, after all. Charles would be home in a week, and they would have seven whole days together as a family.

She used the rare opportunity of having an afternoon to herself to take a hot bath, and then she decided to work on the sweater she was knitting for Bundles for Bluejackets. She made of cup of tea, and found some music on the radio.

Curled up on the couch, she caught a faint whiff of lavender still on her skin from her bath. It was with a sense of loss and longing that she had used up the last drops of her bath oil. She wondered if Charles's sister Kate and her daughters were still making time for such small indulgences as their home-made lavender oil. She doubted it. Two of Kate's sons had already been deployed, and a third was in boot camp, leaving only the youngest son at home. She didn't know how they were going to manage the farm.

Lillian realized that the last truly peaceful time she had known was the summer before the war, when they had visited Kate and her family in the Midwest. And it would surely be a long time, if ever, before she felt such peace again. Her mind was constantly on alert – listening for air raid sirens, steeling herself for the latest news bulletins, wondering if the rationing would get much worse.

She gave a deep sigh and tried to remember that summer on the farm. But it had become increasingly difficult to hold such images in her mind. They were being crowded out by disturbing headlines and worrisome newsreels.

Her hands stopped knitting as she heard someone approach the door. A quick glance at the clock told her that it was early for the boys to be back. She heard keys at the door, and then saw Charles coming in.

"Charles!" she cried, jumping up and greeting him. "What a surprise! You didn't tell me you were coming." She embraced him and noticed that he held her more tightly, and longer, than usual.

"How long can you stay?" She quickly noted the expression on his face – was it worry? Sadness? Something was amiss. "What is it? Is something wrong?"

His eyes quickly searched the room. "Where are the boys?"

"They're out on their salvage drive. What is it, Charles?" She lived in constant fear of another assault on the US, or a surprise invasion. "What happened? Has there been an attack?"

"No. No," he said, and held her again.

She looked him over. "Are you all right?"

He held her gaze for a few moments, and then spoke gently. "It's Gino."

She took a step back and tried to read his expression. "Gino?"

Charles's eyes winced at the pain his words would bring. "His ship was torpedoed. Off Iceland."

She took a quick intake of air. "But – he's all right?"

He slowly shook his head. "There were no survivors."

A thousand pinpricks filled her body. "Oh, Charles! It can't be true. Are you sure?"

"I heard about it yesterday and didn't want to believe it. But I confirmed the findings – and asked for a twenty-four hour leave. I came as soon as I could."

Lillian pressed her hands to her mouth. "Oh, my God. Not our Gino." Tears shot to her eyes and she staggered backwards as the room tilted. She dropped onto the couch.

Charles sat down next to her.

She grasped at the only straw of hope she could find. "But – he was in a convoy, wasn't he? He would have been protected. Maybe – "

"He was. A large convoy. But his ship had engine trouble, and fell behind."

Lillian knew the rest and gave a low groan in response to the revulsion she felt for the wolf packs. So like predatory animals. She hated to think of them preying on sweet Gino. She could see him, fresh-faced, smiling into the sun, or gazing up at the stars, while below the dark waters the pack lurked, encircling, closing in for the attack. She put her face in her hands, and tried not to imagine the rest.

Then her head snapped up, her face full of dread. "The boys – they'll be so hurt. Oh, my God. How can I tell them? How can I tell Tommy? He'll be crushed."

Charles squeezed his eyes shut. As much as it hurt to see Lillian's pain, he wasn't sure how he would handle Tommy's.

"And Anna Mae – he was so happy – " Lillian choked, unable to finish.

Charles drew her to him and stroked her hair, her shoulder. Then he reached into his pocket and pulled out Gino's letters. "He gave these – " his voice broke. "He gave me letters that he wrote to his grandparents, and to Anna Mae. In case…"

Lillian placed a hand on Charles's arm, for the first time comprehending how this news affected him.

He took a deep breath. "I'll deliver them tomorrow, on my way back. They will have been notified by now." He looked at the handwriting that seemed to capture Gino's spirit – his happiness, his earnestness – and then slipped them back into his jacket.

Lillian's eyes filled with sorrow. "What terrible times these are."

Charles shook his head, and rubbed his hands over his face. "It's going to get worse before it gets better."

Lillian saw the fatigue in his face, and realized that he probably hadn't eaten or slept since he heard the news. She caressed his hair, his cheek. He kept his gaze fixed straight ahead, avoiding her eyes. She put a hand to his cheek and gently turned his head to her. "Are you all right, Charles?"

She wondered at his silence. What struggle was going on inside him?

"There's something else," he said softly.

Her eyes searched his face, fearing more bad news.

"I'm so sorry to have to tell you this now." But he couldn't say it.

A fist twisted in Lillian's stomach, knowing what it was. "Oh, my God. You're leaving."

"I received my orders yesterday. I didn't think it would be for a few more months."

"When?" Her voice came out in a whisper.

"The 26th. I have to return tomorrow – but I'll have a week's leave before shipping out." He hoped his last words would offset the bad news, if only a little.

Lillian buried her face in his shoulder, trying to control her trembling.

"It has to be done. We're doing everything we can to avoid more attacks like the one on Gino's ship." He stood now, and leaned against the mantel, his hand clenched at his side. "They've had control of the Atlantic for years. But they're not going to have it for much longer. I can promise you that."

Just then they heard laughter and footsteps running up the stairs. They exchanged a look of apprehension, and then Tommy and Gabriel burst through the door.

"Dad!" cried Gabriel, and he ran to hug him.

"Hello, son," Charles said, hugging him back. "Hello, Tommy," he said, avoiding looking directly at him.

Tommy was spilling over in exuberance from the success of their drive. "Man oh man, did we clean house! We had to make two trips to Mickey's basement!"

"We got a broken jack-in-the-box," added Gabriel, "three golf clubs, and the super of one building even gave us an old garbage can that we rolled back." The memory of the last item caused them both to break into laughter.

They wriggled out of their coats and tossed them on the hall tree. "You should see Mickey's basement. It's getting full. We're gonna win first place, I just know it." Tommy gave Gabriel a playful tap on the head. "Wait till I tell Gino!"

Charles looked away, and Lillian put her hands over her mouth.

Tommy finally realized that something was wrong. That they weren't responding like they should. He and Gabriel traded glances.

"What? What happened?" Tommy stood in front of Lillian. Her eyes seemed all red. "What, Mom? What's the matter?"

Gabriel stood next to Tommy and waited for her answer.

Lillian reached out and took Tommy's hand, but didn't say anything.

He pulled his arm back, angry that no one was telling him anything. "What? Tell us!"

"Tommy," Charles said quietly. "It's about Gino."

Tommy froze, as if poised for an attack. His eyes quickly shot from Lillian to Charles. "What? What about him?"

Charles sensed Tommy's mounting frustration and didn't want to prolong it any longer. "His ship was torpedoed," he said simply. He waited to see if Tommy and Gabriel understood what he was saying. But their faces were blank, expectant. "There were no survivors."

Tommy blinked at Charles, his mouth forming a question. "You mean – No. There must be a mistake! Somebody got something wrong."

"I hoped to God it wasn't true. But it was all confirmed by an escort ship. I'm so sorry, boys. I'm so sorry."

Tommy's mouth started to quiver and his face crumbled, a mix of anger and pain and shock and sorrow. He ran into his bedroom and slammed the door behind him.

Gabriel hesitated, not sure if he should follow. Then he curled up next to Lillian and let her hold him. After a few minutes, he lifted his face to her. "Did it really happen?"

"I'm afraid so." She drew him closer to her.

Gabriel was quiet for several moments. "What about Anna Mae?"

Lillian kissed his head. "I know, honey. It's very sad. Gino left some letters with your father, for his grandparents and Anna Mae. He's going to deliver them tomorrow morning."

"Then will you come back home?" Gabriel asked, his eyes full of fear.

Charles sat next to Gabriel. "I have to go back to Virginia. But I'll be here Christmas week."

Gabriel sat silent, looking down at the floor. "I want to write to them, too. Will you take my letters to them?"

Charles nodded, and smiled sadly at Gabriel.

Gabriel went to the kitchen drawer and took out a notepad and pencil. Then he sat down at the table and wrote his letters.

Lillian leaned into Charles, and spoke in a low voice. "Let's not tell them about your leaving. Let's wait until next week."

She went into Tommy's room. He seemed so small and vulnerable, his shoulders shaking, his face buried in his pillow. There were no words that came to her. She sat next to him, and stroked his hair, bending down now and then to kiss him.

Chapter 9

Izzy leaned against the conference table after the morning meeting at Rockwell Publishing. "I just can't believe it," she said, blowing her nose again. "First there were boys from the old neighborhood I heard about. Now it's hitting closer to home. My cousin Reggie, then my godson Franklin. It's hard to take in. They're a part of your life. You send them off, you get their letters – and then, just like that, they're gone." Izzy put her hand on Lillian's arm. "And now Gino. Makes you want to cry," she said, ignoring the fact that she was crying. "How are the boys handling it?"

"Tommy's taking it pretty hard. He thought of Gino as an older brother."

"The poor kid. What is he – eleven? That's a tough age. Anything I can do?"

Lillian picked up her notebook, and slowly stood. "Thanks, Izzy, but I don't think anything can be done. Time just has to heal him."

"At least Charles will be home soon," said Izzy, as they left the conference room. "That'll help."

Lillian groaned. "We haven't yet told the boys about – his leaving." She found it hard to say – the thought left such a void in her heart. She grasped at the one thing that kept her somewhat lifted. "But he thinks he will be back within a few weeks. This first time. Before leaving again," she added quietly.

"Well, all you can do is make the best of it." Izzy pressed the elevator button. "It's going to be a hard Christmas for a lot of people."

"I know. I'm so grateful that we'll at least have Christmas together. Our first one, you know, as a family."

Just then, the elevator doors opened and Rockwell stepped out. He took Izzy by the elbow.

"Miss Briggs, I want you to organize a meeting for next week. I'll announce the winners of the poster contest then. Make it a kind of " – he waved his arms, searching for what to call it – "a Christmas party. Hang some decorations. Order some snacks or something."

Lillian almost smiled at Rockwell, pleased at any bit of news that took her mind off the war. Every now and then she saw a different side to him that surprised her.

"A Christmas party?" asked Izzy. "Why, Mr. Rockwell, whatever has got into you? Are you feeling quite well?"

"Don't be smart. Just do as I say." He spun around to Lillian. "Mrs. Drooms, I understand you're the last to submit a painting. You do understand that this is more than a contest for prizes. You artists always think the world revolves around you. It's an assignment, and I expect you to fulfill it!"

Lillian watched him walk off, and gave an ironic smile. "Just when I'm beginning to like him, he does something that makes me go back to disliking him. It drives me crazy."

"That's because you're not around him enough. When you see him every day, as I do, you can only dislike the man," laughed Izzy.

*

Lillian stopped by the babysitter's to pick up the boys after work and was alarmed to discover that Tommy was not there. Apparently he had left school and went home on his own.

"I call him two times, and I just call again," said Mrs. Kuntzman. "He says he's fine. Not to worry about him. Mrs. Wilson went to him. Just to make sure."

All kinds of thoughts ran through Lillian's mind. Was Tommy sick? Was it the news about

Gino? He had never done anything like this before. She looked to Gabriel for some sort of explanation.

He hunched his shoulders and put up his hands in ignorance. "He left school after lunch, Mom. I thought he was coming here."

"Well, hurry up – go get your shoes and coat."

"I call him first time when I see Gabriel alone," said Mrs. Kuntzman. "I tell him to come here, that I take care of him, but he says no." She went to the kitchen and came back with a jar of soup placed in a basket. "So I make him chicken soup. With dumplings." She patted her remedy for everything.

"Thank you, Mrs. Kuntzman," said Lillian, taking the basket. "I think it's the news of Gino. It hit Tommy especially hard."

"Ach!" she said waving her hand. "This terrible war! So sad. War takes all our best young men."

Lillian suddenly remembered that Mrs. Kuntzman had lost her son in the Great War. "Oh, I'm sorry – you of all people understand the loss."

Mrs. Kuntzman lowered her head for a moment, softly nodding. But when she looked up her face was full of strength, as if she had briefly drunk from some deep, refreshing well.

"Tell Tommy that Gino is still alive in here," Mrs. Kuntzman said, pressing her gnarled, arthritic hand to her chest.

Lillian looked at the knobby hand against the flour-dusted red apron, the smiling eyes and nearly white hair, and felt a rush of affection for this woman who had become like a grandmother to Tommy and Gabriel – watching over them before and after school, baking treats for them, praising their schoolwork, offering words of comfort.

"And the soup will help," Mrs. Kuntzman added. "Love in a jar. I don't want our Tommy sad."

"I'll tell him. Thank you."

"Bye, bye, Gabriel. You take some soup, too. Make you strong!" The elderly babysitter made fists of strength, and then patted him on the head. Then she leaned over and whispered in his ear: "I put cake in there, too. For dessert."

Just as Lillian was opening the vestibule door to leave, Mrs. Wilson came in. She untied her scarf and patted Lillian's arm. "Tommy's fine," she said. "I took the liberty of looking in on him. I was visiting Mrs. Kuntzman when Gabriel arrived alone. Sad times, sad times." She put her hands on her knees so that her face was level with Gabriel's. "All ready for Santa?" she asked loudly, and pinched his cheek. Without waiting for an answer, she whispered to Lillian. "Tommy'll be fine. Time heals all wounds, they say. Well, I'll let you be on your way."

"Thank you, Mrs. Wilson," said Lillian. "Thank you for looking in on him." Though both women assured her that Tommy was fine, Lillian wouldn't be convinced until she saw him for herself.

She hurried home with Gabriel, and ran up the two flights of stairs to their apartment.

"Tommy?" she said, opening the door. There he was, stretched out on the couch. She pulled off her gloves and felt his forehead. "What's wrong, sweetheart? Do you feel sick?"

Tommy lifted his shoulders and then dropped them. "I did. I'm okay now." He sat up on the couch and put a pillow on his lap.

"Why didn't the school nurse call me?"

Tommy twisted his mouth. "I didn't go to her. I just came home."

"Tommy. Why didn't you call me, or go to Mrs. Kuntzman's? You know that's the plan."

"I know." He kept his eyes on the pillow.

Lillian had never seen Tommy looking quite so lost. She put her arm around him and smoothed back his hair. It broke her heart to see him so sad.

"Did you eat lunch? Are you hungry?" She set the basket on the kitchen table, and then took off her coat and hat. "Mrs. Kuntzman made some chicken soup for you. I'll heat it up."

Gabriel rummaged around the basket and called out from the kitchen. "And she gave us some cake, too. Chocolate!"

Tommy raised himself up, ambled into the kitchen, and slid into his seat at the table. He put his elbows on the table and rested his chin in his hands.

Lillian soon had the table set with bowls of soup and a loaf of fresh bread.

"You know," said Lillian, buttering a slice of bread for Tommy, "Mrs. Kuntzman is very sad about Gino. She lost her son in the last war. He was her only son. She said to tell you that Gino will always live in here." She patted her chest, just as Mrs. Kuntzman had done.

Tommy blew on his soup, and nodded as if he already knew that.

"I think she missed you. She's gotten used to seeing you and Gabriel every day." She noticed that while Gabriel had already dug into his food, Tommy still showed little interest in his.

Tommy gave a half grin, and stirred his soup around.

Gabriel looked up from his soup. "Mickey and Billy asked if we're going on the scrap drive tonight."

Lillian watched Tommy, hoping he would agree to go.

"I don't think so," he said. "My stomach still feels kind of funny."

"Mommy, can I still go even if Tommy doesn't?"

"I think it's best if you stay here. Make sure you're both not coming down with something." Lillian went along with the stomach sickness, knowing that Tommy's ailment fell into that vague but powerful category known as heartache.

She was relieved when Tommy finally ate his dinner. He seemed to perk up a little bit afterwards, helping Gabriel to find a show on the radio, and listening to it with apparent interest.

But the next morning he said he didn't feel good again, and didn't want to go to school.

Gabriel put his hand on his arm. "It's because you're sad about Gino."

"That's not it," Tommy said, pushing away Gabriel's hand. "My stomach hurts."

Lillian put her arm around Tommy. "That's okay, sweetheart. You can stay home. I'll stay here with you."

"You don't have to, Mom. I'm old enough to be here by myself."

"I know that, but I want to make sure it doesn't get any worse. Why don't you go back to bed for a little bit?" she asked, walking him back to his room. "Sometimes a good sleep sets everything to right."

Tommy nodded, and crawled into bed.

Lillian called in to work to say she wouldn't be in. Then she walked into the bedroom, and caressed Tommy's hair. "I'll walk Gabriel to Mrs. Kuntzman's, then I'll be right back."

Lillian let Tommy sleep all morning. She tried to work on her drawing for the contest but had no heart for it. She woke him for lunch, and set him up on the couch. Again, he seemed fine and read his books, dozing off now and then.

In the afternoon, she sat next to him with her sketch pad and made a few strokes. "Gabriel wrote letters to Anna Mae and to Gino's grandparents. Charles said it made them very happy. They told Charles they were grateful that Gino had gotten to know us as a family – and that he finally had gotten the little brothers he always wanted. Isn't that nice to know? Do you think you'd like to write and tell them how important Gino was to you?"

Tommy let his gaze drift away from his book, thinking about it, but didn't respond.

"You know," she continued, "just because someone dies doesn't mean they're gone from your life."

This time he looked up at her, waiting for more.

But she realized she didn't have a ready answer. It was more like a feeling she had always had. She set her sketch pad down, and thought about the people she had lost in her life, and what she had done to remain close to them. She still felt the presence of her mother every day, in a thousand little ways.

"There are ways you can still feel them with you, things you can still do for them. Ways you can honor them."

Tommy gave it some thought, and then went back to his book.

Lillian knew that Tommy sometimes kept things inside, considering ideas, storing away thoughts until the right time came to examine them. For now, it would be best to keep him busy.

She put her sketch pad away, stood up to stretch, and then clasped her hands together. "How about we make a special dinner tonight? Surprise Gabriel."

A little glimmer of light appeared in his eyes, and she knew she was on the right track.

"Will you help me?"

Tommy nodded, and closed his book.

Lillian sat next to him. "What do you think we should make?"

Tommy appeared more animated as he considered Gabriel's favorite meals. A small smile formed on his lips. "Fried chicken and mashed potatoes?"

"Mmm. And there's more of Mrs. Kuntzman's cake for dessert," Lillian added.

Tommy sat up. "He's gonna love it."

"Then we better get busy!"

She found a station on the radio with Christmas music, and for the next hour and a half she and Tommy peeled potatoes, scraped carrots, and prepared dinner. She let him roll the chicken in flour, and she placed it in the frying pan. By the end of the afternoon, they had a large platter of fried chicken and a pan of mashed potatoes with melted butter on top.

It all looked and smelled so delicious that Lillian lifted a drumstick, bit into it, and sighed in enjoyment.

Tommy turned around with his mouth open. "Mom!"

"Just wanted to make sure it tasted all right," she said smiling, and handed it over to him. "You better check, too."

Tommy took his time enjoying it, and nodded. "Just right." He looked over at the mashed potatoes and raised his eyebrows.

Lillian nodded. "We better make sure." She lifted the lid and gave Tommy a spoon.

After a few spoonfuls each, they decided the mashed potatoes were perfect. Lillian replaced the lid, and then covered the platter of chicken and set it in the oven to keep warm. She looked up at the clock.

"Just in time! Won't Gabriel be surprised? Do you want to come with me to pick him up?"

"Yeah," said Tommy. "Let's bring Mrs. Kuntzman some chicken. She always gives us food."

Lillian gave Tommy a hug, and sensed that he was beginning to emerge from his darkness.

As they neared the brownstone on the corner, they saw Mrs. Wilson, who lived two floors above the babysitter, coming out of the building.

"Well, *what* a coincidence!" she said. "Mrs. Kuntzman and I were *just* talking about you, Tommy. Come! We have something to show you." She turned around, marched back up the stairs, and opened the vestibule door. She waited for Tommy and Lillian to come up the stairs, and then knocked on Mrs. Kuntzman's door.

Mrs. Kuntzman came out, followed by Gabriel, and clapped her hands. "Hello, Tommy. Ah! My chicken soup makes you better."

"Look what they made, Tommy!" cried Gabriel.

Mrs. Wilson positioned herself next to a large box in the hallway. "Its permanent place for as long as you're collecting salvage," she said.

Tommy walked over and looked at the box. The words *For Gino* were written above a blue star that was edged in a gold border.

Tommy touched the star and smiled up at Mrs. Wilson, and then at Mrs. Kuntzman.

"We had a little disagreement over the color of the star," said Mrs. Wilson. "I insisted that it *must* be gold, seeing that Gino gave his life for his country."

"But I say it must be blue, because Gino is still here with us," said Mrs. Kuntzman tapping her heart.

"So, they made it both," said Gabriel, opening his arms in explanation.

"This is swell," said Tommy, still rubbing his hand over the box.

Mrs. Wilson straightened and put her hands on her hips. "And *I'll* make sure that the materials are collected properly." She gestured with her head to the floor above and whispered, "I already had to blow the whistle on Mr. Redmond. I caught him adding an unflattened tin can. He won't be making *that* mistake twice. Mark my words."

Tommy laughed, his eyes taking in the star again. "This is really swell. Gino would be happy."

"Well," said Mrs. Wilson, with her hands on her hips. "We must all soldier on. Which reminds me. The spotters are awaiting their supplies. Sandwiches." She whipped out her scarf from her coat pocket and tied it firmly under her chin. "I need to make a quick trip to Mancetti's. Ta-ta!" And with a brisk wave, she was out the door.

Gabriel sniffed the air, and looked wide-eyed at the basket in Lillian's hand. "I smell fried chicken."

"For Mrs. Kuntzman," said Tommy, taking the basket and handing it to her. "Mom and I made it. Just now. And there's some mashed potatoes and carrots, too."

"How nice! Thank you, Tommy." She peeked under the cloth and raised her eyebrows. "Ah! It looks delicious!"

Tommy saw Gabriel's fallen face, and put a hand on his shoulder. "Don't worry, Gabe. There's plenty left for you."

"Then come on! Let's go!" Gabriel cried, and opened the door. "Bye, Mrs. Kuntzman!" he called out over his shoulder.

*

Lillian kept Christmas music on throughout dinner and was happy to see that Tommy enjoyed the dinner as much as Gabriel. He was more talkative, and listened to Gabriel's news about school.

"Billy's making a tin foil ball out of gum wrappers," said Gabriel, "and it's already as big as a baseball. He said when it's the size of a grapefruit he'll give it to us for the drive. And Amy asked about you."

Tommy blinked a couple of times. "What did she say?"

"She said she hopes you're feeling better and that her Mom has a stack of papers for us. And Mickey said the diner was saving tin cans for us. But that we have to flatten them ourselves."

Lillian cleared the table and placed Mrs. Kuntzman's chocolate cake in front of the boys. When they were in the middle of eating the cake, Gabriel suddenly put his fork down, got up, and went to the cupboard. He pulled out his Hopalong

Cassidy lunchbox, and with a bang, set it firmly in front of Tommy.

Tommy looked at the lunchbox, then up at Gabriel. "What?"

"For our drive," said Gabriel. He sat back in his seat and scraped up the last bite of cake.

"Thought you didn't want to give it up."

"That was before." Gabriel took a swig of milk, and wiped his mouth. "Now I do."

Tommy fixed his eyes on the table, and finished his cake in silence. After a few moments, he asked, "Mom, can we go on our salvage drive tonight?"

Lillian glanced at the clock and nodded. "You better hurry."

Chapter 10

Mason decided to walk home from work, as he often did when he needed some time to clear his mind. He didn't like the way he had handled himself with Edith. They had always been close, and lately he felt as though he was reprimanding her too much, finding fault. Was he turning into a crotchety old man? What had she called him – a schoolmarm? That's certainly not how he saw himself.

He liked to think he was a man of reason and compassion. Yet he felt that he was losing control of the family he had spent his whole life keeping together, after his father died. It was true they didn't need him anymore, not like they used to. In part, he was happy about it. He knew that his sisters would make their way in the world; they were all educated, confident, spirited.

But he was afraid the family was fragmenting and that everything was spinning out of control. There was too much talk about handsome soldiers, and dances, and chorus lines, and going off to join the Red Cross or WAVES, or something that would enable them to do their part – admirable, but worrisome. Who would look after them in far-flung corners of the globe? Even his eleven-year-old daughter said she was going to enlist when she was older! The world had turned upside down too quickly for him.

He looked up at the apartment buildings along the street. Every time he walked home he noticed new service stars hanging in the windows. It seemed that a blue star hung in every apartment, sometimes with several stars on the same banner. When he passed a gold star, he felt a sinking feeling inside, and hoped that a sad face would not appear in the window. The loss and sorrow the families must feel was unimaginable.

As he rounded the corner, he bumped smack into a group of rowdy GIs.

"Hey! Why aren't you in uniform?" one of them asked in a slurred voice.

Another one of them stuck his chest out and saluted Mason, causing the others to crumple into laughter. As they propped themselves against each other and moved on, Mason thought he heard them say something about a white feather.

He opened his mouth, about to defend himself. Then changed his mind. What's the use? he thought. They obviously had been drinking, and for all he knew, they were shipping out tomorrow. He couldn't blame them. He watched them stagger down the street, singing some song and laughing uproariously, already forgetting about him.

Mason shoved his hands in his pockets and continued on his way home, trying to ignore the feeling of guilt they had stirred. And yet the sting was there. He felt himself becoming all bad-tempered again, and began to defend himself to himself. He was helping where he could, wasn't he? Purchasing War Bonds through his payroll deduction, filling in as air raid warden and spotter for the men in his building, helping out with his kids' drives and collections, and most importantly, volunteering at the veterans' hospital every Tuesday evening after work – writing letters for the soldiers, bringing them books or reading to them, listening to them, encouraging them.

He just about had himself convinced that he was doing enough, when he thought of some of the individual wounded men he had tended: Carlton, with no legs; Smitty, who jumped at the slightest sound; Big Al, who was struggling with Braille. He let out a deep sigh of inadequacy. It could never be enough. Nothing he could ever do would be enough. How could it be – when they lay there maimed, blind, disfigured, shattered inside? Their lives would never be the same.

He plodded up the stairs to his apartment, and stomped off the snow from his boots. When he opened the door to his apartment, he saw that Alice, Helen, and Claudia were on their way out. Again. Dressed for some party or dance. They flitted around Edith, clamoring to see the ring they had spotted on her finger. She was trying to put them off, but nevertheless appeared amused at their enthusiasm. Seeing the dark expression on his face, the younger sisters grabbed their coats and left hurriedly.

Mason had sincerely determined not to berate Edith anymore, but a ring? He had to say something.

"Edith," he said firmly. "I think this has gone far enough."

"And I don't think it's any of your business." She turned her back on him and reached for her coat.

"I won't stand and watch while my sister is made a fool of." He didn't believe anyone could make a fool of Edith, but he thought that appealing to her pride was the one way to make her see reason.

"I wasn't aware that you had such a low opinion of me. But, however you feel, the way I choose to live my life is no concern of yours." Standing in front of the hall tree mirror, she wound her white scarf around her neck.

"Edith. Wake up! You know he'll leave you for the first pretty actress that comes along. And I don't want to be around you when that happens. I know how you'll react." The expression on her face in the mirror made him wish he had chosen different words.

"I don't blame you," he said more gently. "I'm sure he's charming, and that it's tempting to want some of the excitement his profession brings, but – "

Edith whipped around, her eyes afire.

"Stop, Robert! Before you dig yourself in too deep. You've repeatedly insulted a man you don't know, haven't even had the decency to meet – " she put up her hand when he tried to speak – "but I thought you knew me. You speak as if I'm no better than a senseless schoolgirl, enamored of the stage."

"I didn't mean that. You know what I mean."

"I know that I've tried to please you, tried to hold the family together! There were things *I* wanted to do, opportunities *I* wanted to seek." With each assertion she pressed her hand on her chest. "You have your career, a family of your own. Did you never think that I might want that for myself? Did you never think that *I* want more out of life?"

"Edith, listen to reason – "

"No!" she cried. "I've been reasonable for too long and it has dulled me!" Her hands trembled as she buttoned her coat.

Mason had never seen her so upset, and back-pedaled as best he could. "I've never stopped you. You've always done what you wanted to do."

"How can you say that?" Her face took on a pleading sadness as she turned to him again. "There were things I wanted to do. I had planned and saved for a trip to Europe. But no, the time wasn't right, you said. I wanted to spend a week by the ocean, but again you spoke against it."

"But you always wanted to go alone. I couldn't let you go without any protection."

"I *needed* to be alone – I needed that, to heal. *I* knew what I needed, you didn't. The only word you knew was *Wait*."

"I just wanted you to wait until you were stronger."

"I'm as strong as I ever will be! And I'm not waiting anymore! I want life – I want to feel again. To live again!" She was shaking now, her anguished words mixing with her tears.

"Edith," he said, surprised at her passion.

"Enough! I've had enough! I'll find a place of my own, or move in with Desmond."

Mason didn't believe her threat. "You won't leave us."

Edith fixed him with a wry smile. "Why? You think no one else would want a *cripple*?" She grabbed her hat and left.

That last word, hurled at him with such bitterness, hurt him more than she could know. Mason moved to the living room and watched her through the window. She held onto the railing as she climbed down the stairs – the limp that none of them ever alluded to, breaking his heart.

*

Edith never cried in front of people, and she was furious that she had shown such weakness in front of Robert. She impatiently dabbed at her eyes and lifted her chin. She was through with living according to someone else's will. There was always something more that was wanted or needed or expected from her. She had been foolish. Here she was, in love, really in love for the first time in her life. And she had hesitated when Desmond proposed. She was a fool. But no longer.

She walked to the theater where Desmond was helping out with the rehearsal for the show he was to have been a part of. She tried to leave the argument behind her, but her brother's words had lodged inside, their barbs stuck deep. Did he really see her as helpless and hopeless, with no future but as a spinster? Was life to hold nothing more for her than that?

Try as she might, she couldn't ignore the thought that was most wounding her. His words about Desmond had struck the deepest blow: "He'll leave you for the first pretty actress that comes along." A pretty actress without a limp is what he meant. She hated her brother for stirring the doubt that had lain dormant in her mind. She believed in Desmond's love, in his integrity, in his gentle nature that wouldn't willingly hurt others. And yet. Even a doubt spun of airy imagining can turn into a stubborn, poisonous thorn.

Edith entered the dark theater quietly, not wanting anyone to see her until she had composed herself. She took a row in the far back. There was little heat in the theater and so she kept on her coat and hat and gloves, hugging herself against the chill. Cold and dispirited, she watched the actors on the stage – Desmond reading the lines, the others already off script.

But Desmond had been watching for her, and now, shielding his eyes against the lights, he raised his head in greeting.

Her heart swelled at the tiny gesture. Love would heal her; Desmond would heal her. She was sure of it. She wanted his love to take away the pain of her brother's words – words that still coursed through her veins with tiny thorns, lashing her from inside.

Her mouth softened as she observed him reading his lines. Before she met Desmond, she thought she had been content with her life. There had been a nagging emptiness, but she assumed everyone had such a feeling – for all the dreams that still cried out to be fulfilled, all the dreams that had been shelved. She was no different from everyone else. But as their relationship developed over the months, she found that her dreams were being answered by his smile, his warm eyes, his loving caresses. The future that had once been a dim somewhere else, now shone large and bright, inviting her in a welcoming gesture: Come! it beckoned. A glittering time of happiness awaits you.

Edith closed her eyes in gratitude, and then filled her gaze with Desmond. This man, up there on stage, moving under the bright lights, had pulled back the veil, and shown her how beautiful life could be.

She watched him perform, exaggerating his gestures for the farce. There he was, her Desmond – graceful, strong, illuminated – there, where he belonged, bathed in the glow of stage lights. He was at home up there – just as she was comfortable here. In the shadows, an observer. Perhaps he was right, she smiled. They did complement each other. Complete each other.

The angry trembling in her slowly subsided. She had made up her mind that she would spend the night with Desmond. She would no longer care what anyone else thought, except him.

She heard the lobby door open and close, and a burst of light briefly flooded the aisle as the curtain next to her parted and then closed. There stood a beautiful young woman, stylishly dressed in a shimmery gold coat and hat. Unaware of Edith, she watched the actors, smiling, clutching her collar to her chin. When the scene ended, she clapped her hands. "Bravo!" she cried, and then ran down the aisle and up the stairs to the stage.

A flurry of greetings and hugs surrounded her. A fellow actress, no doubt. Wide arms and a big embrace from Desmond. "Valerie!" He was happy to see her. Edith had never seen him so happy.

When the man at the piano broke into a playful tune, Desmond and the actress began to dance, hands linked – then Desmond dipped her backwards, and – a kiss? Some number they had apparently performed together, many times. Then laughter, applause, cheers from the others. The beautiful actress, naturally dynamic and fascinating in her moves, held them all rapt.

Edith's chest began to rise and fall deeper and faster, and a shivering coldness crawled over her. She waited for Desmond to remember that she was there. To perhaps introduce her to the actress and explain away the obvious.

But the beautiful woman was now recounting some story, using her hands, sweeping her arms wide in a dramatic fashion, holding them all spellbound. Then at the conclusion of her tale, she clapped her hands together and tossed her head back in laughter, causing the others to howl with merriment. Desmond also found her amusing, enchanting. The woman linked her arm with Desmond's as they strolled around the stage. He placed a hand over hers, and listened attentively. Enamored.

Edith sat invisible, her lips pressed tight together, but still trembling, as she watched the scene that her brother had just so cruelly predicted.

From a silent place inside her, from their place, Edith called out to him – willing him to look her way. "Desmond!" her heart cried out. Her heart cracking, fracturing, splintering as the cry went unanswered.

Up there on stage a story was playing out, a couple deep in conversation, a couple who looked so right together. And she, Edith, was merely an audience member, silently watching the scene. The young woman commanded attention without even trying. She tossed off her hat and coat onto the stage couch. The stage lights favored her, played with her, catching on her golden hair, reflecting off the shimmer of her silk dress that swirled with each step. Graceful, lovely. Beauty inhabited the stage.

Edith realized how dull she was in comparison. To all the women he was forever surrounded by. Why should she be surprised at what she was seeing? The only thing to surprise her was that she had been so naïve – that she had foolishly begun to mistake the dream for reality. She hardened herself, and took one last look at the stage. At the handsome couple. At Desmond. And then she quietly left the theater.

As she walked through the falling snow, she pushed the image of Desmond and the woman out of her mind. And focused on Robert. At that moment, she was angrier at her brother than she had ever been before. She couldn't face him. She couldn't let him know that he had been right. She inhaled deeply, enjoying the cold, sharp air that lashed at her lungs.

She spent the next several hours stopping by apartment buildings and boarding houses, searching for a room. It was good to be back, to be awake again. Good to close the door to that fairy future and once more move among the solid gray shapes of the present workaday world. It was good to have known a pretty dream – and good to have wakened from it. She was back on firm ground.

After knocking on countless doors, and speaking with numerous people, she realized, with a sinking heart, that there was nothing to be found. All apartments were full to capacity. Unless she wanted to cram into a room full of young, cheerful, chatty women, which she couldn't bear. Her threat had been empty. Again, as Robert had predicted.

She would swallow her pride and go home. At least she had her own room there, a room where she could be as alone as she wanted.

The black night pressed down on her, reminding her that it was late. She was exhausted and her leg was hurting, throbbing with each step – deep stabs reminding her of past sorrows, unkind twists of fate. She shook off those old remembrances and turned the ache into an ally, into something that would help to steady her on the long, low road ahead.

She made her way back home, climbed the steps to the apartment, and closed the door behind her, awash with weariness and the heavy burden of defeat.

Chapter 11

⌒

Lillian set a bowl of parmesan cheese on the table, and then stirred the pasta boiling on the stove. She inhaled the aroma of the spaghetti sauce and garlic bread and glanced up at the clock. Charles would be home soon, and would be there for Christmas week. Nothing would mar their last days together before his leaving. Except that tonight they would have to tell the boys about his departure. They would get it over with, and then do their best to make it a happy Christmas.

Her eyes traveled over the kitchen and living room – everything appeared festive, cozy, and welcoming. The table was set, and dinner was ready. The living room was softly lit by the single lamp behind the couch and the glow of the multi-colored lights of the Christmas tree. The tinsel and ornaments reflecting the lights added a touch of sparkle.

The boys sat in front of the tree, also awaiting Charles's arrival. Predictably, Tommy was wearing his old red sweater, and Gabriel wore a pale blue vest over his shirt. She was curious to know if they would like the new sweaters she had purchased, in shades of green, and brown, and white.

Tommy sat curled up on the couch, tapping a pencil on a tablet as he worked on his Christmas list. Gabriel hummed along with "Santa Claus is Coming to Town" from the radio as he crawled around the floor, rearranging the wrapped presents that lay under the tree.

"Gabe," said Tommy. "We have to start our Christmas shopping. How about we start with The Red String Curio Store tomorrow?"

"Okey dokey. Are we going to get you-know-what, for you-know-who?" he said, pointing his head towards the kitchen, where Lillian was draining the spaghetti. "Those cards?" he whispered in answer to Tommy's puzzled face.

Just then the door opened, and Charles came in, all smiles. The boys immediately noticed the long box in his arms.

Gabriel ran over to him. "Hi, Dad! What's in the box?"

"Hello, son!"

Tommy got off the couch and walked over to him.

Charles mussed his hair. "Hi, Tommy. What are you two boys up to?" he asked, as he took off his coat and hat.

"Just making our Christmas lists," said Tommy.

Charles noticed the presents all spread out. "You're not peeking, are you?"

"No," both boys laughed.

Charles handed the box to Tommy. "It's kind of heavy. Why don't you put it under the tree? We'll open it after dinner."

"What is it?" asked Gabriel. "Is it for me too, or just Tommy?"

"It's an early Christmas present. For all of us."

Charles went to the kitchen and wrapped his arms around Lillian. "It's good to be home!" He noticed the carefully set table with a green and red checked holiday tablecloth, and a platter of gingerbread and a pudding sitting on the counter. "That must have depleted your rationing book," he said, still holding her tightly.

"Almost." Lillian sank into his warm embrace. "I'm so glad you're home."

Gabriel was right at his side again, unable to suppress his curiosity over the box. "Can you tell us what it is?"

"After dinner," said Lillian. "We'll have dessert and open our first Christmas present. Come, sit down."

Over dinner Charles and Lillian kept exchanging glances, in acknowledgment that Tommy seemed himself again. He and Gabriel recounted their success with the salvage drive, and their plans for the holiday, starting with some Christmas shopping the next day.

"Can I have some more, Mom?" asked Gabriel, holding up his plate.

Lillian smiled to see her boys eating with such appetites. Tommy was already on his second helping.

"It kind of feels like Christmas this year," said Gabriel, "and it kind of doesn't. Cause of the war. Can I have some more milk, too?"

"Yeah," said Tommy. "It feels too dark, for one thing. Christmas should be bright."

"Well, the dim-out isn't making our home any darker," said Lillian, refilling both their glasses. "Just look at all our lights and decorations. And our beautiful tree."

"You know," said Charles, taking another helping of pasta, "there's an advantage to having a darker sky."

Both boys waited for him to say what it was.

"Like what?" Gabriel finally asked.

"You can see the stars better," explained Charles. "The next few nights are supposed to be clear. That means we'll be able to see the Geminids meteor shower a lot better."

"What's that?" asked Gabriel, with a mouthful of pasta.

"It's a meteor shower that takes place every year around this time. We're at the tail end of it, but with the darker skies, it should still be visible. We should see a whole host of shooting stars."

Tommy suddenly sat up. "A telescope! You got us a telescope!"

Charles nodded, delighted that Tommy was so excited about it.

"Can we open it now?" asked Gabriel, pushing back his chair.

"Not in the middle of dinner," laughed Lillian. "I didn't know you two were so interested in astronomy."

"It's because of Gino," said Gabriel. "He knew everything about the stars. From being a sailor."

"Yeah," said Tommy. "He told us how you can steer by the stars. First you have to find Polaris, and then you can figure out where you are."

"That's the North Star," explained Gabriel.

The energy level of the dinner was boosted with talk of falling stars, and constellations, and how a telescope works.

An hour later, they were all in the living room, Tommy and Gabriel taking bites of plum pudding in between listening to Charles read the instructions, and then handing him the pieces he pointed to. The telescope was almost assembled.

"We can look at the stars every night," said Gabriel. "Hey, we could have a New Year's Eve party on the roof. Remember that time in Brooklyn, Mom, when we all went up to the roof on New Year's?"

"Can we, Mom?" asked Tommy. "The spotters would be happy about that."

Charles caught Lillian's eye, and saw that she gave him a small nod to proceed. "That's something I wanted to talk to you boys about."

Tommy had seen the exchange between them and was on high alert. He tried to read his Mom's face, but she had her eyes fixed on Charles.

Charles set the instructions down, and rested his eyes on Tommy and Gabriel.

"I've received my orders to ship out. I'll be here all week, but I have to leave right after Christmas. So I won't be here for New Year's – but you can have the party without me, and then tell me all about it when I get back." Try as he did to minimize the news, the boys stared at him with open mouths, their eyes full of fear. He tightened a screw on the telescope and picked up the instructions. "I don't think I'll be gone for too long this time, but it looks like I'll have to leave more often from now on."

Gabriel looked around at everyone, and then lightly shook his head. "Uh – I don't think you should go. I think you should tell them you can't. Maybe later."

Tommy blanched and stood up. "You can't go. Mom, tell him he can't go."

Lillian began to stack the plates on the coffee table. "Now boys, you know he doesn't have a say in the matter."

"You knew, didn't you, Mom?" Tommy asked angrily. "Pretending that everything is normal, and that it's going to be a good Christmas." He whipped around and addressed Charles. "You can't go! You don't have to go. You're too old." He crossed his arms in front of him.

"I *do* have to go, Tommy," Charles responded gently.

Tommy released the long-suppressed words inside. "No! You're just saying that! You could have stayed here with us. With Mom. That's what she wanted. We were supposed to be a family. We finally got a dad and now you're leaving us!"

"Tommy – " Lillian started to explain, but he cut her off.

"It was supposed to be different! Better. It's worse!"

"Tommy!" Lillian scolded.

"What? My real dad would have stayed!" He spun around and headed for his bedroom.

Lillian sat up. "Thomas Hapsey!"

Silence filled the room. No one moved.

Tommy slowly looked over his shoulder at her. "Hapsey?" he sneered. "See, Mom? Even *you* don't think of him as my dad."

Lillian jumped up from the couch, about to light into him, but Charles placed his hand on her arm. "Let him go. He doesn't mean it."

Lillian brought the dishes to the sink and began washing them with a loud clatter. She was angry at Tommy's behavior, angry that she had used her old married name when she yelled at him. And she was disappointed that her carefully planned evening was not turning out as she had hoped.

Charles took up the instructions, but after staring at them for a few minutes, he set them down, and went to Tommy's room.

"Go away, Mom!" Tommy started to say, but then he saw that it was Charles. He sat up and hugged his knees, waiting to be lectured.

Charles stood next to Tommy. "You all right?"

Tommy nodded but kept looking at his feet, his face scrunched up in defiance.

Charles lightly placed his hand on Tommy's shoulder and felt that he was all tense and tight – an adolescent bundle of anger and fear. Charles sat down next to him.

After a few moments, Tommy shifted a bit, and let out a deep breath, as if he had been holding it. Charles noticed that he had dropped the hard look, and some of his tenseness was gone.

"Sorry," Tommy said, almost in a whisper.

Charles shook his head, as if it didn't matter. "Tommy, the day I married your mother, and we all became a family, was the happiest day of my life. There were so many things I was looking forward to. Moving to a house. Family trips. Baseball games. All of us being home together in the evenings. But we're at war. And I have to do my part."

"I know that," said Tommy. "But I still don't want you to go." His voice began to quiver. "I don't want anything to happen to you." He roughly wiped away the tears that had spilled onto his cheeks.

"Tommy, you know I can't talk about my work with the Navy. But if we want to win this war, we *have* to keep our shipping lanes safe. It will mean that fewer men like Gino will die."

Tommy bowed his head and sniffled. He wasn't going to cry. He wasn't. He sniffed hard and sat up straighter.

"You really have to go?" he asked, for the first time looking up at Charles.

Charles smiled at the sweetness in Tommy's face, and saw that his eyelashes were clumped together with tears. He was torn between wanting to hold him like a child, and treating him like the growing boy he was trying to become. "Yes. And you'll be in charge, once again. Think you can handle that?"

Tommy nodded. "You can count on me."

Charles put his arm around him. "I know I can. You're doing your part in this war, and I couldn't be prouder of you. Helping your mom and Gabriel. Helping our servicemen with the salvage drive. Helping me, so that I can do my job."

Tommy gave a smile with one side of his mouth.

"We're going to get through this war, Tommy," Charles said, feeling that they had turned a corner. He watched as Tommy pulled at a button on his cardigan and twisted his mouth, as if struggling with something. Charles squeezed his shoulder. "So, we're okay?"

Tommy gave a slow nod, and bit his lip in indecision. "Can – can I ask you something?"

"Sure, you can."

Tommy looked up again with that sweet vulnerability that melted Charles. "How come you never call me *son*?"

Charles had to look around the room for an answer. "Don't I?"

"No. You call Gabriel *son*, but you just call me *Tommy*."

Charles was kicking himself for being so insensitive, and tried to pin down why what Tommy said was true. "I don't know. You so rarely call me *dad*, that I guess I wasn't sure you wanted me to."

"I thought maybe it was because you like Gabriel better than me. Everybody loves Gabriel.

He's always happy." Tommy nearly pulled the button off his sweater as he explained. "I get in bad moods and say things I don't even mean. Gabriel makes everybody happy. " He gave a little smile. "Even me."

"Aw, Tommy, that's not it at all. You have different personalities, but one isn't better than the other. I love you both the same. And I think of you as my son. That's how I refer to you when I tell anyone about you."

"You tell people about me?" he asked, raising his face.

"Sure!" he said, lightly hugging him. "Everyone I work with knows that I have two sons. And that one of them is really good at baseball, and is doing a heck of a job on his salvage drive."

Tommy grinned and leaned into the hug.

Charles gestured towards the door. "How about we finish putting the telescope together so we can look at the stars tomorrow? It's supposed to be a clear night. If we're lucky, we'll get quite a show."

Tommy smiled and scooted off the bed. "You think Gino can see the stars – wherever he is?"

Charles gave it some thought. "I like to think so."

"Is that why you bought the telescope? So that we think of Gino and his star?"

"In part," Charles said mysteriously.

Tommy looked up at him for the rest of the answer.

With a glint in his eye, Charles added, "And I thought it might make a good science project. With the right partner."

Tommy's eyes widened as all the gears clicked into place. "For my class! Oh, man, wait till I tell Amy that I have a real telescope! Think I can show it to her tomorrow?"

"Sure," said Charles, as they walked back out to the living room.

"Mom!" cried Tommy, rounding the corner. "I finally know what my science project is going to be! The stars!" Then he saw the look on her face, and remembered his earlier words. "Sorry, Mom," he said in a subdued voice. "I told Dad I was sorry."

That he had referred to Charles as his dad made Lillian suddenly very happy. She held Tommy close to her and kissed his cheek. "My darling boy!"

He briefly put his head on her shoulder and then looked up. "Can I show the telescope to Amy tomorrow? It's supposed to be a clear night."

"Let's have a stargazing party up on the roof!" said Lillian, drawing Gabriel to her other side. "With hot chocolate to keep everyone warm. I was going to bake cookies tomorrow anyway. How about we make some of them star-shaped and hand them out to the spotters?"

"We'll help you decorate them, Mom," said Tommy.

"Maybe Amy would like to come early and help decorate them, too," she suggested.

Tommy's face lit up at all the wonderful things that were suddenly happening to him.

"Can I call her and ask her? Now?"

Before Lillian could say yes, Tommy had dashed for the kitchen, with Gabriel right behind him.

"Tell her about the cookies," Gabriel said. "Tell her to come early to help us."

As Tommy dialed the number, Lillian smiled at Charles in gratitude.

"Hey, Tommy," they heard Gabriel say, "we can put three stars together and make an Orion's Belt cookie!"

*

In the middle of the night, Lillian woke from a deep sleep with the sudden clarity of the image she would paint for the poster contest, seeing it in perfect detail. She shivered in the cold as she crept out of bed and slipped on her robe.

She quietly went into the living room and turned on the lamp behind the couch. There was the telescope, pointing up, as if in readiness to search the heavens. She was glad for the stars, for their high, untouched beauty that could not be sullied by war, by humanity. She took out her sketch pad and pencils and began to draw.

It didn't matter what Rockwell or anyone else thought of it. It was a drawing that she had to make – for Gino, for Tommy, for herself, for Charles – for anyone yearning for hope and love in the darkness.

Filling the sketch pad she drew two separate night scenes – a small town and a smoky battle-field – both under a starry sky. On one side, a young woman leaned against a porch railing, holding a letter and gazing up at the stars; on the other side, a dying soldier lay propped against a tree, clutching his side. He also held a letter in his hand, and beheld the same stars.

Lillian studied the drawing, holding it out at arm's length. "No," she said, resting it on her lap again. She erased a few lines and redrew the soldier. Not dying. Wounded. There must be hope, she thought; hope that our men will come home. I can't live in a world without hope.

She added more stars to the skies, trying to convey the belief that high above a war-torn world, the glittering firmament shone benevolently over earth, and that in the end, all would be well and whole again. Simple, humble, human love would help to piece the world back together again.

For another half hour she filled out the drawing, envisioning the colors she would use. She would take it into work and finish it in watercolor and ink – it would be both sharp and soft, dark and illuminated.

She closed her sketch pad, and turned off the lamp. And then tired and cold, but filled with tranquility, she slid back into bed, next to her warm, safe husband.

Chapter 12

Mrs. Sullivan paced about the office of Drooms and Mason Accounting, turning something over in her mind. She had noticed a change in Edith for the past few days, and was sure it had to do with her young man. Desmond had actually stopped by the office the day Edith called in sick, desperate to talk to her – and since then he had called several times. Each time Edith had stepped out of the office, saying to take a message.

There was no denying it; the light had gone out of Edith. She smiled and was pleasant to all, but there was a different air about her – resignation. That was the sentiment she exuded. And there was a decided coldness between Edith and her brother.

When everyone left for the day, Mrs. Sullivan, never one to pry, nevertheless determined to ask Mason about it when he returned from his outside meeting. She suspected that he had a hand in whatever had happened, and was prepared to speak her mind.

Mrs. Sullivan had worked herself into a state, her heart breaking for the sensitive young woman. When Mason came in, she scarcely waited for the door to close before launching into her questioning.

"Mr. Mason. It may be none of my business, but I feel that I *must* speak. Whatever is going on between you and Edith has taken a toll on her."

Mason hadn't even gotten out of his coat and hat, and was taken aback by the unexpected attack – not least because he had also noticed the change in Edith, and felt responsible. Though he had used harsher words with her than intended, he still believed he had done the right thing and that she would soon come to her senses.

He set his briefcase down on his desk, opened it, and took out a few papers. "She'll get over it. She's just letting me know that she's angry with me." He hoped his simple explanation would put an end to Mrs. Sullivan's interference, well-intentioned though it may be.

But she was not to be so easily put off, and followed him to his desk. "I think it's more than that. Her young man has called here repeatedly – twice today, and she won't take his calls. What on *earth* happened? I've never seen her like this. She's keeping up a good front, but I know a broken heart when

I see one." When he didn't respond, she pushed him a little further. "You didn't say anything to discourage her, did you?"

A flash of guilt crossed Mason's face. "Well, for her own good, yes, I did say something." He didn't want Mrs. Sullivan to make more of it than it was. He began to shuffle through the already opened mail, and spoke in a casual tone. "I'm afraid I told her to break it off."

Mrs. Sullivan threw her hands up. "Well, if that doesn't beggar all belief!" she said, her cheeks flushing pink. "Edith is a grown woman. She has proven herself to be a level-headed business woman, she's been an ideal role model for your younger sisters. You yourself said she's been working since she was sixteen, she's educated. Good gracious, what more do you want of her?"

Mason had opened his mouth twice to speak, but Mrs. Sullivan wasn't finished.

"And now she's found someone she loves and who loves her. Hasn't she earned the right to that? Why would you want to come between her and happiness?"

Mason jerked his head back at the accusation. "How can you think such a thing? Her happiness is *exactly* what I'm trying to protect."

He held up a hand before she could get in another word. "Mrs. Sullivan, with all due respect, I know my sister better than you do. You've only known her for the past year." He didn't feel it was his business to speak about Edith's personal life, but neither did he want to be charged unfairly.

Mrs. Sullivan raised her chin and folded her hands in front of her, patiently waiting for the words that would explain away his interfering handiwork.

Mason sat down and let out a deep sigh. "In part – or maybe wholly – I'm responsible for what happened to her, when she was young. There was a time when – She was so devastated when – "

Mason rubbed his forehead and looked at the cracks in the floorboards. Where to start? The memory that came to him softened the line of worry that forever creased his brow. "You didn't know her, before. Before the polio, she was more like her sisters – high spirits, fun-loving, more outgoing." He waved his hand at her whimsical nature. "She used to write poetry. Sew costumes for herself and the girls. They all went swimming in the summer, skating in the winter. She always had that dreaminess about her, but she was so – " Mason searched for the word that would describe the old Edith – "*enamored* with life."

"And then she contracted polio," said a softer Mrs. Sullivan.

"No." It took Mason a moment before clarifying. "And then *I* contracted polio."

"*You*, Mr. Mason?" Mrs. Sullivan blinked at the information. She had worked with him for over twenty years, and never knew of this.

"Yes. And Edith was my nurse. She never left my side. There wasn't enough she could do for me." He lifted and dropped his shoulders. "Apparently, I had a mild case. I recovered. But then Edith came down with it. Hard. And the doctor and everyone feared that it would sweep through the house. So they quarantined her. Hired a nurse. Edith had a difficult time of it, but eventually she recovered. She underwent it all with remarkable stoicism – because she was in love and was going to be married." He waited a few moments before adding, with a hardened tone, "To my best friend, Jack Mittford."

Worse and worse. "Oh, Mr. Mason. I *am* sorry." Mrs. Sullivan sat down at this point, knowing that the tale was not going to be a pretty one.

He looked down at the floor again, remembering Edith's young face. "She was in love as only a young girl can be – with dreams of the future, of marrying him and having children. The wedding was planned. The girls were involved in it. We were all so happy. She had made it through the illness, and was ready to pick up where she had left off."

Again he put his hand to his forehead and rubbed it, as if warding off a headache or some unpleasant thought. "I met Jack at college. He had a promising future ahead of him. Was fun-loving. I thought he loved Edith."

He slowly nodded, confirming the details with himself. "And then one evening, about a month after her recovery, Jack stopped by the house. To see me. I could tell he had been drinking, I guess to make what he had to say easier. At the time, Edith's limp was more pronounced, and it looked as though she might have to walk with the help of a cane. Ole Jack started to hint that he wanted to break off the engagement. Said Edith needed some time. I could see what he was getting at. We began arguing. I didn't realize that Edith had returned home from the doctor, or I would never have raised my voice."

"And Edith heard?" asked Mrs. Sullivan, dreading the answer.

"She was there – on the staircase. She heard everything Jack said. I'll never forget his words: 'she's not the same girl I fell in love with. Come on, Robert – you can't expect me to marry a *cripple*.'"

Mrs. Sullivan groaned. She knew the proud young woman well enough to know how deeply the words would cut her.

"A cripple!" said Mason, freshly outraged. "In one fell stroke he had reduced my sister, our wonderful

Edith, to something to be shunned, pitied! *My* heart broke when I heard those words – to describe Edith as some wounded thing of no value. I lost my head and began shouting, and Edith quietly stepped into the room – still so pale, so fragile – yet stony in her resolve. 'Robert!' she cried. 'Let him go.' She held his gaze, with him squirming like the worm he was, until he hurried out."

Mrs. Sullivan's eyes blazed with anger. "The worthless scoundrel! I'd like to find him and box his ears!"

It was a few moments before Mason could pick up the story.

"After that, she closed down. She never said a word. Never shed a tear. But we all saw the results of sleepless nights. She grew thinner and thinner. There was a point where I began to fear for her life. She pulled through, and put up a brave front. But our old Edith was gone."

Mrs. Sullivan placed her hand over her heart. "Oh, the poor, dear girl."

Mason took a deep breath and let it out. "The other girls have had heartaches and disappointments – they cry and mope and go a few days looking all wrung out – and then they bounce back. But Edith feels things more deeply. She always has. And now to see her full of that girlish happiness again, getting her hopes up, with an *actor*, for God's sake. What chance of happiness does she have?"

"And yet it *is* a chance! Give her credit for opening herself up again, for allowing herself to hope. Unlike you, I've met the gentleman – he's a lovely man, with integrity and honor. Of course, I could be wrong – but don't we all take that chance with love?"

Mason shook his head. "I couldn't bear for her to go through that again. To get hurt again."

"Oh, Mr. Mason, you're such a worrier. To quote someone or other: 'A ship in harbor is safe – but that's not what ships are for.' Let her weather the storms, and get tossed about by tempests, but for heaven's sake, let her sail!"

Mason studied the floor again, considering her words.

Mrs. Sullivan took the hankie from her sleeve and blew her nose. "Enough of all this. You've blamed yourself for long enough. Time to butt out of Edith's affairs and let her live her own life." She sniffed again. "You do know he's shipping out soon to entertain the troops."

Mason looked up sharply. "No. I didn't know. That must be why she's so subdued."

"He's putting himself in harm's way. There's never any knowing what will happen over there, who will come back. It's best not to have any regrets."

"You're absolutely right, Mrs. Sullivan. As usual," he added with a smile. "I'll talk to her. Set things right."

"I'm glad to hear it. And forgive me if I spoke out of turn."

"No, no. I'm glad you did. I've been in a bit of a quandary lately, unsure of what to do, how to handle this whole thing."

Mrs. Sullivan rose to her feet and began to gather her things. She lifted a large bag from beneath her desk, and set it down as she reached for her coat. "Well, I'm off to the department store."

Mason leaned forward on hearing the jangle of bells, and caught a glimpse of bright red and fluffy white fabric poking out of her bag. "Mrs. Sullivan – is that a Santa costume in your bag? I thought you said Brendan was sick."

"He's down with a cold. Putting in long hours at the shipyard, and in general behaving like a man half his age. So *I'll* be playing Santa tonight, and every night until he gets better." She noted the surprise in Mason's eye, and added, "I'm not the first female Santa this year, with all the men away or working. Though, if I may say so myself, I'm a bit more believable than most."

"That's very commendable of you," said Mason, clearly amused by the idea.

"We can't let the little ones down. Christmas will come whether we're ready for it or not. And, if truth be told, I rather enjoy it."

Mason chuckled as he imagined Mrs. Sullivan in the Santa costume. "You must be quite a sight in your red – "

"No comment, thank you, sir." Mrs. Sullivan started to leave, but did an about face at the door and thrust out her chin: "The show must go on, after all. As Mr. Desmond Burke might say."

Chapter 13

❧

Tommy and Gabriel had emptied their banks and were now on their way to The Red String Curio Store.

Gabriel twirled around every lamppost they passed, singing bits and pieces of Christmas carols in between talking to Tommy. "So we know what we're going to get for Mom. What about Dad?"

Tommy screwed up his mouth. "I don't know. Gino got him that piece of scrimshaw. That was a good idea. Maybe we'll find something about the ocean, or sailing."

The little bell rang when the boys opened the door to the shop. The Red String Curio Store was one large labyrinth of assorted items from the past one hundred years, full of treasures to some, junk to others. It was more crowded than the boys had ever seen.

The old store owner wore his Victorian red and green brocade vest, in honor of the season. "Hello, boys! Anything I can help you find?"

"We want to get our Mom some of those old-fashioned cards," said Tommy. "Like old Christmas cards. For her collection."

"She's an artist," added Gabriel, "and likes that kind of stuff."

"Ah, yes. I seem to remember you bought her some Valentine's Day cards last year. Come this way. We have a wide selection. Postcards, for the most part."

He walked down one aisle, then up another, and stood still for a moment, getting his bearings. Then he made a sharp right, and then a left, and came upon two old wooden filing cabinets with narrow, deep drawers. He lowered his glasses to the end of his nose and pointed to the labels. "I haven't gotten around to alphabetizing them, but everything is arranged by subject matter, for the most part. You might have to poke around a bit."

He opened a drawer and read a few tabs. "For example, here we have The World's Fair – 1904, that is. St. Louis. And here's Niagara Falls. Horseless Carriages." He gave a little chuckle at one of the images, before closing that drawer and opening another. "Travel. You should take a look at this drawer, if you get a chance. There's a remarkable world out there." He moved to the second cabinet and ran his finger over the labels. "Aha! Here we are – Holidays and Celebrations!"

He pulled out one of the long narrow drawers and read off different tabs. "Easter. Halloween. Fourth of July. Hmm," he said, getting to the back of the drawer. "Bastille Day. Guy Fawkes Day – only three cards in that one. No. Not there." He shut the drawer with a bang, and slid open the drawer next to it, his face brightening. "Ah! Here we are – Christmas!" He pulled out the drawer and set it on a rickety old table for the boys to look through. "Just holler if you need anything," and he disappeared back into the labyrinth.

"Okay, thanks." The boys looked at each other, and then started to sort through the drawer.

Tommy began to read off the tabs. "Boxing Day. Christmas Trees. Yuletide – "

"You sound just like him," said Gabriel. "Maybe you could get a job here."

Tommy pulled out postcards one by one, and waited for Gabriel to say yes, no, or maybe. They ended up with a stack of twenty cards, most of them depicting rosy-cheeked children, snowy villages, and prettily-dressed ladies. Then they searched around and found two old piano stools close by, sat on them, and began to narrow down their choices.

"They all look alike after a while," said Tommy, looking at yet another Victorian maiden with a bunch of holly in her arms.

"No, they don't," said Gabriel. "Look, this lady is skating. This one is holding a wreath. And this one is hanging some – "

"Okay, okay, just pick out the best ones."

They finally decided on six cards. Gabriel put the rest back in the drawer. "Mom's going to love these," he said. "Hey, look! Here's one about 'Father.' Maybe Dad would like it." He began to read: "'Here comes Father Christmas. Come meet him, boys and girls.'"

Tommy peered over at the card and frowned. "That's about Father Christmas, Gabriel. He's like Santa."

Gabriel cocked his head and studied the image. "I like Santa better. He's fatter and looks like more fun."

Tommy turned suddenly to Gabriel. "But that's a great idea, Gabe! Maybe we can find a card for Dad."

They ran their fingers down the remaining drawers, and found a label marked *Family*. They opened it, and after *Mother*, there was a small selection under *Father*.

Tommy pulled out an assortment of about fifteen cards. "Not much to choose from. Father Time. Father's Day."

Gabriel grabbed at a card, amused by the drawing of a portly old gentleman standing on his head. "How about this one? Listen:

'You are old, Father William,'
the young man said, 'And your
hair has become very white; And
yet you incessantly stand on your
head – Do you think, at your age,
it is right?'
'In my youth – '

"Gabriel, that's from *Alice in Wonderland*,"
Tommy said. "We can't give him that. How about
this one? 'Father dear the years are passing with
their pleasures and their cares.'" He wrinkled his
nose. "Nah. Too mushy." He stuck it back in the
drawer.

Gabriel continued reading the rest of "Father
William," laughing at the end of each stanza.

Tommy found a Father's Day card from the
1920s of a man fishing. Another of a man playing golf. He put them back in the drawer. Then he
found a card that read simply, "Father." A tall tree
with rocks around its base rose alongside the edge
of the card, next to a tranquil lake. In the middle
was a poem written in an old-fashioned script.
Tommy read the first line. "'A rock of strength
to lean upon in time of joy or stress.'" He looked
doubtfully at Gabriel.

Gabriel shrugged, and read the next line. "'An
understanding, loyal soul, A heart of tenderness.' It
kind of sounds like Dad."

Tommy read the last lines. "'A mind all wisdom, knowing how justice and love to blend; A teacher, loving, patient, kind. My Father and my friend.'"

They looked at each other for a few seconds, blinking and considering. "Do you think it's too sappy?" asked Tommy.

"Kind of. But I think he might like it."

"Me, too." Tommy cracked his knuckles as he studied the card. "Okay. Let's get it," he said, secretly elated that he had found such a perfect card. It said exactly what he felt – *my Father and my friend*.

"Let's get 'Father William,' too," said Gabriel, clasping his hands under his chin – "please? It's funny. He'll like it. Please?"

Tommy rolled his eyes. "Oh, all right."

Gabriel gave a little hop of joy, and then thinking they had finished with their shopping, he started back to the counter.

But Tommy held his arm. "Wait, Gabe."

Gabriel jerked his head back. "You're not going to get *my* present here, are you? I want something new."

"No, not for you. For Amy. Remember what Gino said?"

Gabriel nodded. "Oh, yeah. You have to get something that shows you were listening."

Tommy's face filled with worry. "And it has to be something – special. That she'll like."

"How about a necklace?" asked Gabriel.

"Nah."

"Perfume?"

Tommy shook his head.

"Well, what kind of things does she talk about?"

Tommy twisted his mouth. "She talks about her family. About school. How she wants to be a scientist when she grows up."

"So let's find something about science."

Tommy bit his fingernail, and then nodded. He looked around the maze-like store. "We better split up."

The boys wandered down the aisles individually, bending down to look in the glass cases, moving objects on the shelves to see what was behind them, rummaging through boxes of miscellaneous objects.

Gabriel rounded a corner and bumped into a black-shawled mannequin – and gave a cry of alarm when it turned around and addressed him.

"Hello, little boy!" said a very old woman, smiling and bending down to his level.

"Hello!" Gabriel cried over his shoulder as he hurried into the next aisle.

After another turn or two, Gabriel came across a shelf full of used science objects. He read the spine of a dusty chemistry book, and was just lifting an old Bunsen burner to inspect, when he heard Tommy call out to him.

"Gabriel! Come quick! I think I found something."

Gabriel ran down one aisle, then another. "Where are you?"

"Over here! In the back."

"Where?"

"Here!"

Gabriel followed Tommy's voice and finally found him sitting on an old upturned crate, looking at something that appeared to be a map.

Tommy lifted his face, a big satisfied smile lighting up his eyes.

"What is it?" Gabriel looked over at the map – and then gave an intake of surprised delight. "The stars!"

"It's a book on constellations, with this pull-out map. It tells when you can see them, and which hemisphere they're in."

"It's science. That shows you were listening!" Gabriel said, amazed that everything had worked out just like Gino said it would.

"Hey, look!" Tommy pointed to a constellation, the connecting lines to the stars making the outline of a man, with three bright stars in his belt.

"Gino's star!" exclaimed Gabriel.

"'Orion, the Hunter,'" read Tommy. "'The Orion constellation lies in the northern sky, on the celestial equator, and is visible throughout the world.'" He ran his finger under the description, stumbling over the names. "'Its brightest stars are Rigel – Beta Orionis, and Betelgeuse – Alpha Orionis.'" He looked up at Gabriel, his face in awe of all this new-found knowledge.

Gabriel gave a firm nod of his head. "You found the perfect gift, Tommy. Amy's going to love it! Gino would be proud of you."

Tommy's mouth curled in his half-smile. "You think so?"

"Yep."

Tommy jumped up from the crate with the book tucked under his arm. "Come on. Let's bring our stuff to the counter. Then what do you say we stop off at the soda fountain on our way home? Get a sundae or something."

Gabriel opened his eyes wide. "Hooray! Ice cream!" He looked up at Tommy. "I scream! You scream!" He waited for Tommy to finish the lines.

"We all scream for ice cream!"

Tommy's heart swelled at the thought that his gifts were going to make so many people happy. He draped his arm around Gabriel's shoulder and they paid for their gifts, thanking the little old man for all his help.

"I'm happy you found what you were looking for," the store owner said, wrapping the book in green paper and then tying it up with red string. "Merry Christmas, boys! Glad tidings, and all that!"

"Merry Christmas!" said Tommy, hugging the book to his chest.

"Glad tidings to you, too!" hollered Gabriel, causing Tommy to laugh as they left the store.

Gabriel resumed his twirling around lamp-posts and singing Christmas carols all the way to the soda fountain. After a few lines of "Good King Wenceslas," Gabriel ran to catch up with Tommy.

"Hey, Tommy – What's the Feast of Stephen?"

Tommy opened the door to the soda fountain for Gabriel. "I don't know. Let's ask Dad. He'll know. He knows everything."

Chapter 14

Edith pressed her hand to her head, and restlessly set aside the newspaper that was filled with news of the war. She then spent a few minutes trying to engage with her book, but was unable to focus her attention. Christmas music and laughter floated upstairs from the living room where her sisters and mother were sewing costumes for the hospital show. Giggles and cries of delight sounded from the kitchen where Susan and the children were piecing together a gingerbread house. It was the Saturday before Christmas, and spirits were high. All as it should be.

Usually, Edith was grateful for the cheerfulness of her family, but today it only accentuated the dismal state of mind that she couldn't shake.

When her sisters called up to her a second time to come and join them, she set her book down and decided that she would go for a walk. She didn't want to disappoint them by declining again, and yet she wanted to be alone. Though she was good at hiding her emotions, she felt that her presence would be a dark cloud hovering over their happiness. And there was the issue of Robert; he had gone into work for a few hours and would be home soon. She would just as soon avoid him.

"Going out, Edith dear?" her mother asked, as Edith passed by in her coat.

"Just a quick walk in the park, and then a little shopping," she said, ducking out before they could press her.

The day was cold but sunny enough to add a bit of warmth, so she made her way to Central Park, thinking the fresh air would help to clear her thoughts.

Yet as she walked, her mind remained mired in shadowy gloom. The relentless news of the war weighed down on her; the world seemed to be slipping into malevolent chaos. She wondered if human nature would ever rise to the heights that were possible, or if its darker side too much enjoyed the lower urges that prevented it from soaring. And would her own nature be forever fraught with weakness and doubt, struggling to rise, only to stumble and fall again? Perhaps that was simply the way of the world. Perhaps life thrived on tension and conflict, and peace was just an idle dream, some illusive, distant beauty – worth striving for, but not worth achieving.

She shook away such thoughts. Though she was at a low point, she would heal and strengthen and become whole again. She knew how to do that, had long ago developed the skill and was confident she could summon it at will. So why haven't I? she asked. What's different about this time?

She stopped on the snow-dusted path and lifted her head, as if listening for the answer. She had the feeling that this time she was not being honest with herself. And without her truth, she could not see clearly. Clarity. That's what was missing. She sighed, and resumed walking, only now looking about her.

Though she had intended to take a different route, she nevertheless found herself nearing the Castle, every turn reminding her of Desmond and their time together. She gave in to the impulse, and climbed the stone steps that led up to the Shakespeare Garden, and continued up to the Castle.

She crossed the courtyard at the base of the tower, and walked over to the stone wall, resting her elbows on it. There was the pond, down below, ringed in snow-covered boulders and withered, dry cattails. Stretched out before her lay a snowy expanse, and farther out, a smudged line of bare trees marked the horizon. She peered far away, past the trees, past the skyline. Beyond lay a world weeping with war, and all around sat heartbreak and sorrow. She closed her eyes and resolved to get through the coming weeks, the holidays, the months ahead.

Her mind was off in a lonely gray dimness, when from down below came the laughter of children. A group of boys and girls played at some game, making designs in the snow. Others made snow angels, moving their arms and legs as if in flight, and then jumping up to see the result. Her lips lifted in amusement as they began to throw snow at each other, falling down in the drifts, oblivious of the cold.

A father walked by with a small child on his shoulders; they stood in front of a snowman and the little child leaned over to pat it.

On the path below, a soldier in uniform linked arms with a young woman. They paused to kiss, and embraced tightly before continuing on.

Approaching from the other side, came an older couple walking arm in arm. They stopped to watch the children, the man gently squeezing the woman's arm. Edith wondered if they were reminded of their own children. The woman laughed, and briefly rested her head on his shoulder. Then they resumed walking, moving with the ease and familiarity of long years together.

Such tenderness and love in the world, Edith thought. How could I have forgotten?

She beheld the scene below, thinking – until recently, I was a part of all that. I belonged to that world. With a sense of loss, she understood how profoundly happy she had been. Why had she so easily given up? She had always thought of herself as a fighter, someone who did not give in to adversity. And yet, she had all but run away from Desmond – and worse, did not give him a chance to explain, at least to hear him out. He had repeatedly reached out to her, but she had refused his calls. She hated to admit it, but in that respect she was exactly like Robert. Making a hasty judgment and then stubbornly holding to it.

Edith looked out over the snowy world, and knew that there were only two choices for her: life with Desmond, or life without him. It was as simple as that. She recalled her life before she met him – going to work, helping with the children, her sisters, nights at home with her books. It was a familiar, secure world, one that had served her well. A small, safe world with a closed door.

Then Desmond had entered her life and shown her a dazzling world beyond the door, a rich wide world, with moments of exuberance and excitement, alongside even more cherished moments of quiet togetherness.

Of course it also meant the unknown, and risk – risk of heartache and disappointment.

Maybe the actress was an old love. Maybe there would be others from his past, or even one from the future, who would cause her pain and sorrow. But she would take that risk.

Even as she steeled herself against a possible onslaught of actresses, some part of her indignantly rejected the idea. The part that believed in Desmond and knew that he was true and that his love was deep.

She filled her lungs with the pure winter air. And in a moment of profound clarity, she realized that it was she herself who had placed the limits on her life – not Robert, or Jack, or the polio. She had allowed her deeply buried insecurities to pin her to the ground, and keep her from the soaring heights of love and happiness.

Enough of that, she thought. That locked way of living is now behind me. In a gesture of release, she raised her arms up and out, as if releasing a captive bird.

Late afternoon lay before her all golden and rosy in the slanting sun, with shafts of light interspersed with shadows of blue and gray among the rocks and trees below.

With her shoulders straightened, and her chin raised, she embraced her new resolve. She would take the risk of pain and sorrow, but she *would* live. She would choose to live in the bright, happiness-infused world that Desmond had opened to her, come what may.

Edith looked down again at the couples strolling and the children playing in the snow. She smiled to hear their laughter ringing in the clear cut-crystal air, and to see the gilded light spread over the earth. She pressed her hand to her chest and thought, how beautiful it all is. How beautiful is human love! How glorious this winter day!

Her heart beat faster and her breath came quicker. She could feel herself coming to life again. She wanted Desmond. Nothing else mattered. He is my love, she thought, whatever twists and turns our path may take – this is my love, and I will treasure and protect it.

She hurried back down the stairs. She would go to him. He would understand.

*

Desmond walked quickly on his way to Edith's home. Though she had asked him not to call on her there, he went against her wishes, fearing that perhaps she was ill.

What other explanation could there be? He stopped momentarily, on remembering that she had gone to work, for he had called there, only to be told that she had stepped away. He picked up his pace again. Perhaps not ill, exactly, but something had made Edith suddenly turn from him. He had been so sure of her feelings for him.

He replayed their last few times together. Surely she hadn't misinterpreted the old dance number with Valerie. Though it was possible. When he had afterwards brought Valerie to introduce her to Edith, he discovered that she had already left – and hadn't given it another thought until after the rehearsal when she still hadn't returned. Or had her brother finally prevailed on her to break it off? He thrust his hands deeper in his pockets. He would get to the bottom of that, too.

He tried to remember what he had last said to her, what could have possibly been misconstrued. Was it that he was leaving soon, and she didn't want the heartache of waiting? Or had someone else entered her life, some old love come back to claim her? And yet, he was sure of her love for him. He must find her.

*

Mason arrived home and felt cheered by all the bustle and laughter that filled his house. This was the way he liked it, everyone busy with some Christmas activity. He would prepare himself a cup of coffee, sit in his armchair and pick up *Nicholas Nickleby* – read smack in the middle of it all. He chuckled inwardly, remembering where he had left off in the book, with the Infant Phenomenon.

In the living room, his mother sat reading a review of their *Fractured Follies* show to his sisters, who sat on the floor cutting fabric and pinning patterns to pieces of red satin.

He popped his head in the kitchen and hugged his wife as she directed the children on decorating the gingerbread house, their hands and faces smudged with white icing. Everyone was in the holiday spirit.

"Where's Edith?" he asked.

"She left about half an hour ago," answered Susan. "To go on a walk. She had that faraway look in her eye."

A stab of regret shot through him as he remembered Mrs. Sullivan's words – that she knew a broken heart when she saw one.

"Robert, dear!" cried out his mother. "We need the hamper from Edith's room. Can you fetch it for us?"

"Top shelf in the closet!" added Alice.

He climbed the stairs and saw that the door to Edith's room stood ajar. A book lay open on the bed, next to a rumpled velvet throw, as if she had decided to leave suddenly.

He found the hamper, an old picnic basket full of remnants of fabric and trim, and lifted it down. He was just about to leave, when he noticed the edge of a small notebook between the bed and nightstand. He supposed it had fallen and he bent to pick it up.

The pages opened to drawings and writing – reminding him of the notebooks Edith used to fill when she was younger. Had she taken up her old habit? He briefly flipped through the pages and saw that they were full of fragments, sketches, words, and smudges of color that meant something to her.

He opened to the latest drawing: a sundial in a snowy garden. A castle tower with the words beneath it: *My kingdom for a kiss.*

Other pages showed a sketch of bare trees. A lamplit bedroom. *Colors of midnight.* Words scattered seemingly randomly on the pages: *Longing. Perchance to Dream.* A flight of stone steps. A hand that beckoned. *Husband. Till it be morrow.* All impregnable to him, though no doubt having to do with her Shakespearean actor.

He was just about to replace the book, flipping back to the earliest pages, when he saw an image that arrested him – an image he immediately understood, as he hadn't the others: a slender white bird, something like an egret or crane, staked to the ground, but trying nevertheless to lift off. A red gash on its white neck where the restraining rope cut.

He knew it was wrong to look at something so personal, but here was a glimpse into the heart that Edith never revealed to anyone. The words written below the struggling bird pierced him.

I wanted to Soar
But loving cords kept me Bound to Earth
Neck straining, Wings flapping futilely
Eyes fixed on the beckoning blue Sky

A wash of pale blue hovered above the bird, a blur of green beneath it. Anguish in the eye of the trapped creature.

Was it *him* keeping her bound to earth? Is that what she meant? His stomach clenched as he mentally defended himself against the words. Hadn't he been helping her all these years? Had he been mistaken? Was she so wounded?

He closed the book and carefully placed it back where he found it.

He walked down the stairs with the hamper. Edith was forever a mystery to him. She inhabited a world of her own that he had no business trying to influence or shape. To think that he had tried to hold her back – that she had perceived his intention to protect as cruel restraint – cut him deeply.

I can't know her heart, he thought. Only she can. She knows what she's doing. And it's not my business. Any more than what happens between me and Susan is hers. How could I not see that? How could I have intruded into such a personal, delicate space? The sacred space of love belongs to the lovers – not to the outer world. What can out-siders possibly know?

He placed the hamper at the feet of his mother, and then went to the kitchen to find Susan. He pretended to be interested in their progress with the gingerbread house, but in truth, he just needed to be next to her, anchored in her. He understood her and her ways. She was a part of him. He could only hope that Edith would find the same.

He kissed Susan's cheek, thinking that he should have listened to her, should have trusted her impression of Edith's young man. She had met him at one of the *Fractured Follies* rehearsals, and couldn't say enough good about him.

The doorbell rang. Susan was icing the roof and held up her hands, indicating that she couldn't get the door.

"There's someone at the door!" Claudia hollered from the living room.

"I'll get it," he hollered back. "I'll get it," he said to himself, walking down the hall.

When he opened the door, he immediately knew that the man standing there was Desmond Burke. And yet the image did not correspond with the one in his head. Here was no dashing young man with a goatee, wearing a doublet, and sporting a rapier at his side. The man before him was close to this own age, perhaps older, with graying temples.

The man extended his hand. "Desmond Burke. I'm looking for Edith."

His manner was courteous, refined. Mason took the extended hand. "Robert Mason. Edith's brother. Come in, come in." He held the door open for him to enter, but Desmond remained standing.

"Is she here? Is she all right?"

Mason noted the worry in the man's eye, and felt a twinge of guilt. "She's gone out. About an hour ago. For a walk."

Desmond didn't want to intrude any longer in the place Edith had asked him specifically not to come to.

"Thank you," he said, and turned to leave, descending the steps.

"Mr. Burke!" Mason called after him. He waited for him to turn. "She often walks in the park."

Desmond tried to read the look on her brother's face. He had expected to be treated rudely, to be told to stay away. This man seemed warm, welcoming, obliging even. "Thank you," he said again, and hurried off in the direction of the park.

Mason closed the door, and stared down at the tile in the hallway. He liked the man. And he seemed to suit Edith somehow, to match her in some hard to define way – just as Susan had said. He should have known that Edith would be level-headed in her choice – that for all her wistfulness, she was at heart, clear-sighted. Yes, he had to admit, the man was well-suited to Edith.

"Who was it, Robert?" Susan asked, poking her head around the kitchen door.

Mason met her question with a sad smile, wondering how he could have been so wrong.

*

Desmond was relieved to know that at least Edith wasn't ill. That provided some peace of mind. But if that wasn't the reason, then there must be someone else. Perhaps someone from her past had resurfaced, and sought her out. And that's why she was avoiding him. Not wanting to give him pain. Hoping he would figure it out. He crossed into the park, and dismissed that thought – it just didn't sound like Edith. There was an unflinching directness about her – at least before all this.

The light was fading; soon it would be dark. He let out a deep sigh, his breath white in the wintry air. He hadn't thought she would go walking on such a cold day, reminding him once again, of how wholly unpredictable she could be – in some things. When it came to her heart, however, he still believed her to be unwavering, steadfast. Surely her avoidance of him stemmed from some simple misunderstanding that they could clear up.

He cut through the park, revisiting some of the places they had been to – the Castle, the

Shakespeare Garden, the fountain, a flight of snowy stone steps that seemed to mirror his lonely state. Evening was settling in now. The gloaming revealed the soft glow from lamplights in the deepening shadows. Should he go back to her house? Should he go home and try to call her?

Over and over, he replayed their last few nights together. Had he been mistaken in their closeness? No – everything was fine until the evening at rehearsal. He needed to see Edith's face in order to understand, to hear her voice.

It was several hours since he had left his apartment, and he was now cold and weary as he climbed the steps and unlocked the door. The thought that he had perhaps lost Edith weighed down on him, making him forget why he had been so happy of late. Why he had trusted himself to that sunny future? Hadn't his past taught him that the only sure thing in life was loss?

He unlocked his door, cursing the cold; his apartment was like ice. He was just about to light the stove to boil some water, hoping a cup of tea would help to warm him – when he noticed Edith's rose-colored coat draped over the living room chair. And his heart leapt. Beat wild and high in his chest.

He walked to the bedroom, and pushed open the door. The light from the hallway fell on Edith's sleeping face, illuminating her like a painting in a museum. She was dressed, but with half the covers pulled over her. He knelt down next to the bed, clasped her hand and kissed it.

"My Edith," Desmond whispered.

She dreamily opened her eyes and smiled up at him. "I was so cold," she said simply.

"Oh, my God, Edith, I thought I had lost you." He wrapped his arms around her, almost weeping with relief. Then he leaned back and studied her face. "Did I hurt you somehow? Did I do something wrong?"

She shook her head and pulled him to her. "No, Desmond. I've been in a foolish place, is all. I'm sorry to have doubted you."

Desmond crawled in next to her, and pulled the covers over both of them. "You doubted *me*? I thought maybe *you* were leaving me."

Edith pressed next to him and laughed. "What a pair we are. I thought you had changed your mind about me."

"Never," he said, holding her close to him. "Never." He drew back and searched her face. "But why did you think that?"

Edith shook her head, embarrassed by her earlier thoughts. "That beautiful actress. She would turn any head. I thought – "

"Oh, Edith. I was afraid you might have thought something like that. I keep forgetting that you don't always know – that you haven't been around the theater and artists and – "

"But I can imagine, Desmond. I can imagine that romances blossom and die with the productions. How could they not? I don't even care. As long as I have your heart."

Desmond smoothed her hair. "I would never be disloyal to you. It's not my way. My Edith," he said, kissing her again.

"But you were so happy to see her. And she is beautiful." Edith let out a sigh and shrugged. "And she dances without a limp."

"Oh, Edith. Your limp is a part of you and I love it. It's part of your mystery and otherness that I so love. Yes, I was delighted to see her. We all were. We all played in a show two years ago. It was a wonderful cast. A wonderful run. One of the best I ever had."

Edith couldn't help regretting that there was so much of his history that she didn't know. She wanted nothing more than to start building her own memories with him. To be able to say – yes, I remember that show. It *was* wonderful.

"Who is she?" asked Edith, wanting to fill in any gaps in her understanding of Desmond.

"Valerie Robbins. A British actress."

"Were you – a couple, once?"

"No, Edith," Desmond laughed. "She's – well, it's not a secret that – " He smiled at Edith's beautifully naïve lifted face.

"What?" she asked.

"She's not interested in men."

Edith opened her mouth, then sat up, peering into the dark room. "Truly?" she asked, trying to make sense of it. "But she's so beautiful. She could have any man she wanted."

"And yet she's been unlucky in love. She's always recovering from some heartache. The last I heard it was a Russian countess."

Edith's eyes grew wider.

"Not that she talks about it. It's understood – we accept it, don't make much of it. In the theater we're used to things being not what they seem. The boundaries are more blurred. Nothing is black and white, or absolute." Desmond gave a little smile. "You're shocked. But I was raised in the theater. It's all normal to me."

"No, Desmond. I'm not shocked. Well, perhaps a little," she conceded, lying back down. "I had imagined a passionate relationship between you two, complete with details. No, I'm not shocked. To me it is refreshing. The openness, the blurred boundaries as you say. To me, it feels expansive, as if you step in and out of possibility, as if the magic of other worlds is woven into all your lives."

"Well, while we're on stage, that's true enough. But off stage – we're just everyday people with failed loves, scrambling for rent, wondering what to fix for dinner – all rather prosaic, I'm afraid."

"No. It's a wondrous world. You live many different lives, and are exposed to other ways of being. I've lived a rather sheltered life."

Desmond cupped her face in his hands. "To be absolutely honest, part of your allure, my dear Edith, is that you are *not* of that world. I know exactly what I have in you. Everything about you is right here – in your sweet face. No airs, no pretense – you've no idea what a comfort I find in that. I know I'm on solid ground with you – I need that. With the shifting grounds of my trade, you're my North Star – steady and bright. I was adrift until I found you. The idea of not having you would be like cutting a boat loose without oars or sail."

He kissed her forehead, her eyes, her cheeks, her mouth. "And you are more exciting than anything I've encountered on the stage. You are through and through lovely and mysterious and exotic and other-worldly. You *are* the thing that we actors pretend at."

Edith threw back her head and laughed. "What a romantic you are. My Desmond." She impulsively took his hand and kissed it, and placed it over her heart.

"Let's celebrate tonight!" said Desmond. "Let's celebrate that we were both wrong, and that nothing has changed, and that we're going to be very happy together for a long, long time."

Edith tossed back the covers, got out of bed, and began to undress. "Wonderful! I'm starving! But first, a hot bath."

Desmond sat up, surprised. "Now?"

"I've been freezing all day. It's the only way to warm up. Come. Let's take a bath, and then go to that little French cafe down the street."

Desmond smiled to think that Edith was by far the more impulsive, dramatic, dreamy one. And that she had no notion of it made her all the more charming to him.

Chapter 15

❧

Lillian rode the elevator down to the Christmas party where the winners of the poster contest would be announced. She knew her submission would most likely languish in the file room; nevertheless, she felt good about it, and was happy that she had simply listened to and followed her heart.

Along with several other employees, she entered the main office and had to stop to admire the transformation. A party atmosphere pervaded the large open room. The office vibrated with the buzz and excitement of the last day before the holidays, conversation and laughter filling the air. From the ceiling hung colorful streamers, and cheerful Christmas music played from a phonograph. Platters of Christmas cookies, a coffee urn, and a punch bowl lined the far credenza. Next to it, a raffle table was set up, with a crowd gathered around it, examining the various items, which included several War Bonds. In the back of the room, next to Rockwell's office, the draped easels were being arranged by the head of the Art Department.

Lillian knew that Izzy was behind most of the planning, including the spiked punch. Rockwell had told her to organize the holiday party, and Izzy had run with the idea, convincing him that a War Bond raffle would reflect well on him. Izzy moved about the room, giving last-minute directions for the raffle and the poster contest. Lillian noticed that she was wearing the red dress she had so admired in the window a few weeks past.

Rockwell made his entrance, and the room quieted while he delivered a few stiff words of thanks and holiday good wishes, and the need to work even harder when they returned after Christmas.

Then he moved to the platform with the covered easels and waited for the crowd to gather around him. With little ceremony, he unveiled the third prize poster, Izzy rolling her eyes at his utter lack of flair. Lillian knew that if Izzy had been in charge of the contest, she would have whipped off the veil in a dramatic reveal, amidst much cheering. Rockwell moved on to the second place and first place winners, handing out envelopes and shaking hands.

Though the themes were predictable, Lillian had to admire the composition and execution of the fighter planes, and the sinking U-boat – though she thought the pairing of a wounded soldier next to Uncle Sam, best of buddies, was a bit of a stretch. She wondered why there was a fourth canvas.

Rockwell moved to the fourth easel and pulled off the drape – revealing Lillian's poster of the soldier and his girl gazing up at the stars.

Her mouth dropped open to see her painting so exposed. Was he going to reprimand her in front of everyone? Say that it was too "sweet" and make an example of her for not following instructions? Several heads from the Art Department turned to her, and she felt the color rise to her cheeks.

"The panel of judges, and myself, have decided to give an honorable mention to Mrs. Drooms. This theme," he said, waving his hand over the painting as if it were somehow problematic, "well – it's not what I asked for, but it works."

A round of applause went out to all the winners, and the level of conversation soon rose to its previous level, with most people either stopping off at the punch bowl to refill their cups, or moving over to the raffle table.

Izzy walked over to Lillian, and gave a light shrug, indicating that she had no idea about the honorable mention. "Congratulations."

They moved closer to the paintings where a few people lingered. Lillian turned a questioning eye to Mr. Rockwell.

"Thank you, sir. I was afraid you wouldn't like it."

He uttered a kind of grunt, suggesting that in part, she was right. "You'll be getting the February cover – a special Valentine's Day edition on the importance of – well, love in wartime and that sort of thing."

Izzy jerked her head back, and fixed him with an exaggerated stare of concern.

Rockwell waved his unlit cigar at her. "Yes, yes, it's sentimental, Miss Briggs, but trust me – it will sell."

Izzy was pulled away to tend to the raffle across the room, and Lillian began to follow her.

"Mrs. Drooms," Rockwell began, "a moment please."

Lillian recognized his scowl of annoyance. "Yes, sir?"

"You got talent – but sometimes I wonder if you know it." He gestured to the winning posters. "Look at these three paintings. Tell me what you see. What do the winners have that yours doesn't?"

Now for the lecture, thought Lillian. She studied the other drawings. "Well, the winners have themes of battle and destruction – and heroism, of course," she was quick to add. "Mine – is on a smaller scale, between two people."

Rockwell lifted his eyes to the ceiling, impatient. "What else?"

"Well, these are done with bold strokes, vibrant colors – reds, orange, black." She glanced over at him to see if she was on the right track; she wasn't. "And dynamic images of smoke and fire and – "

He waved his hand against her words. "All that is artist stuff. I'm a nuts and bolts kind of man. Meat and potatoes. Dollars and cents. You're still missing one big point, and until you get it, you won't be taken seriously as an artist."

Lillian looked in dismay, and swallowed. Again and again, she compared her painting to the others. "Well, mine has a female figure in it. Perhaps it is overall more feminine. Too feminine? Is that it?"

Rockwell uttered a heavy sigh of exasperation. "I thought you artists were supposed to be observant." He flicked his fingers on the winning posters, making a snapping sound as they hit the canvas, and read the artists names as he went. "Steinmeyer. Harrison. McKenzie."

Then he tapped Lillian's drawing. "No name. Blank. What does that tell a panel of judges?" He raised his eyebrows while he waited for an answer, then scowled. "Sign your work!"

Lillian's mouth remained open. "Well, I thought perhaps it wasn't that kind of competition. I thought – I mean I didn't think – "

Rockwell cut her off. "Like I said earlier, Mrs. Drooms, it's a good thing I'm not paying you to think!" He stuck the stub of his cigar into his mouth, and left for the other side of the room.

*

Lillian laughed as she recounted the incident to Charles the next morning, as they lingered in bed. She lay on her stomach, propped up on her elbows. "I didn't know whether I wanted to give him a kick or a hug."

Charles laughed along with her, and then kissed her shoulder. "The main thing is that your work was recognized – as it should be. I knew you would come up with something meaningful."

"I'm afraid you had more belief in me than I did." She suddenly stopped and sniffed the air. "Did you already make the coffee?"

"No – I thought you had."

Their brows creased in perplexity, and they quickly got up and dressed. They went to the kitchen and were startled to see Tommy flipping a pancake, and Gabriel setting the table.

"We're making breakfast!" Gabriel announced.

Tommy looked up from the stove, and exchanged a grin with Charles.

"It smells wonderful," said Charles. "What are you making?"

"Pancakes, toast, and coffee. And hot chocolate with marshmallows," Gabriel said, pointing to the table, which was crowded with jars of jam, jelly, honey, and maple syrup.

Lillian saw that strands of tinsel and a few ornaments had been borrowed from the tree and now decorated the table. "What a wonderful surprise!" she cried, giving both boys a big embrace.

Over breakfast, Tommy and Gabriel talked about what had happened at school the day before, and how Skippy Petrie's team had won the salvage drive contest.

"His dad owns a grocery store," said Tommy, "so he gets a lot of cans and papers and stuff. But I don't care. We came in second."

"And we had more fun the way we collected," said Gabriel.

"We sure did," laughed Tommy, remembering their antics.

The bitter coffee and lumpy pancakes didn't prevent the breakfast from being one of the most delicious Lillian had ever tasted.

*

Later that evening, Tommy and Gabriel, with the help of Amy, finished decorating the last of the cookies, while Lillian filled several thermoses with hot chocolate and coffee. Then they all bundled up to join Charles, who was already up on the roof setting up the telescope and talking with the spotters.

Lillian was buttoning up her coat when she suddenly stopped, went to her bedroom, and came back out – with the brooch from Gino glittering on her collar.

"The star pin!" cried Gabriel.

Tommy stood before her, his eyes taking in the brooch. Then he looked up at her, and a smile of understanding passed between them. Lillian gave him a quick hug, and then they gathered up the thermoses, and followed Gabriel and Amy up to the roof.

"Come on, Amy!" cried Gabriel, running up the last flight of stairs. "We'll show you Gino's star!"

The rooftop was rarely so full. The regular spotters were up there, along with Billy and Mickey, Mrs. Kuntzman, Mrs. Wilson and her husband, and a few other neighbors. Lillian offered cocoa and coffee to everyone, while Amy and Gabriel passed around the tins of fresh-baked Christmas cookies, star-shaped.

Tommy walked away from the crowd, and over to a quiet corner on the roof. He gazed up at the starry sky, and found Orion's Belt.

"Thanks, Gino," he said softly. "I'll always remember you."

Then he looked over at the man who had helped him time and again, never giving up on him. The man who believed in him, who had become his teacher, father, and friend. And who made their lives so happily complete.

Tommy walked over and stood next to Charles, and smiled up at him.

"Thanks, Dad."

Charles wrapped his arm around Tommy, and steadied the telescope as he fixed it on the stars.

Made in the USA
Monee, IL
28 October 2023